D0966935

Mighty Mighty MONSTERS

The KING of HALLOWEEN CASTLE

STONE ARCH BOOKS
a capstone imprint

Mighty Mighty MONSTERS

The KING of HALLOWEEN CASTLE

created by Sean O'Reilly
illustrated by Arcana Studio

Mighty Mighty Monsters are published by Stone Arch Books, A Capstone Imprint
1710 Roe Crest Drive, North Mankato, Minnesota 56003 *www.capstonepub.com*

Library of Congress Cataloging-in-Publication Data
O'Reilly, Sean, 1974-
The king of Halloween castle / written by Sean O'Reilly ; illustrated by Arcana Studio.
p. cm. -- (Mighty Mighty Monsters)
Summary: The Mighty Mighty Monsters must relight the flame of Halloween or else the haunted holiday will no longer be scary.
ISBN 978-1-4342-2150-6 (library binding)
ISBN 978-1-4342-3419-3 (paperback)
1. Graphic novels. [1. Graphic novels. 2. Monsters--Fiction. 3. Halloween--Fiction.] I. Arcana Studio. II. Title.
PZ7.7.O74Kin 2010
741.5'973--dc22 2010004119

Printed in the United States of America.
032018 000236

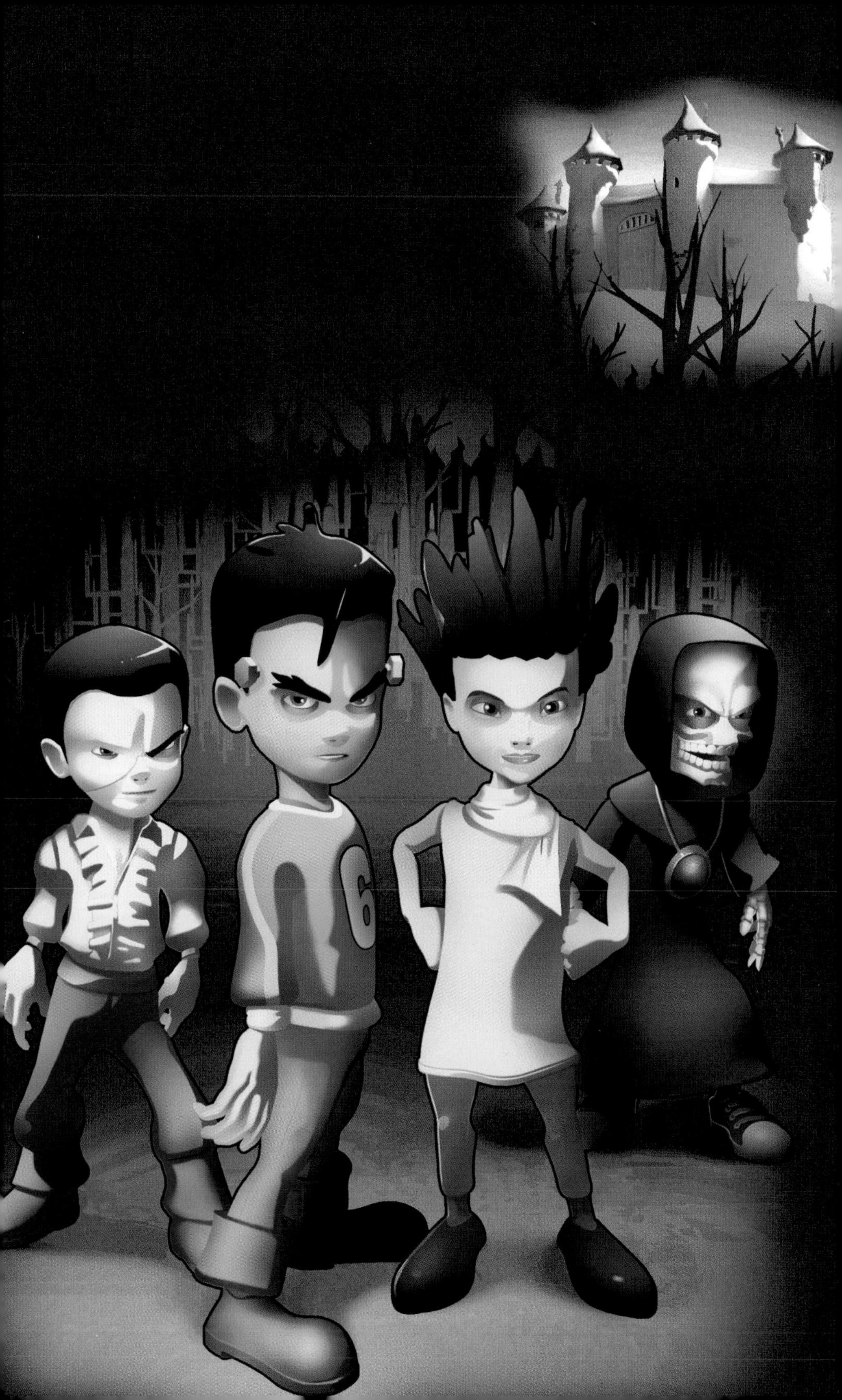

In a strange corner of the world known as Transylmania . . .

Legendary monsters were born.

WELCOME TO TRANSYLMANIA

But long before their frightful fame, these classic creatures faced fears of their own.

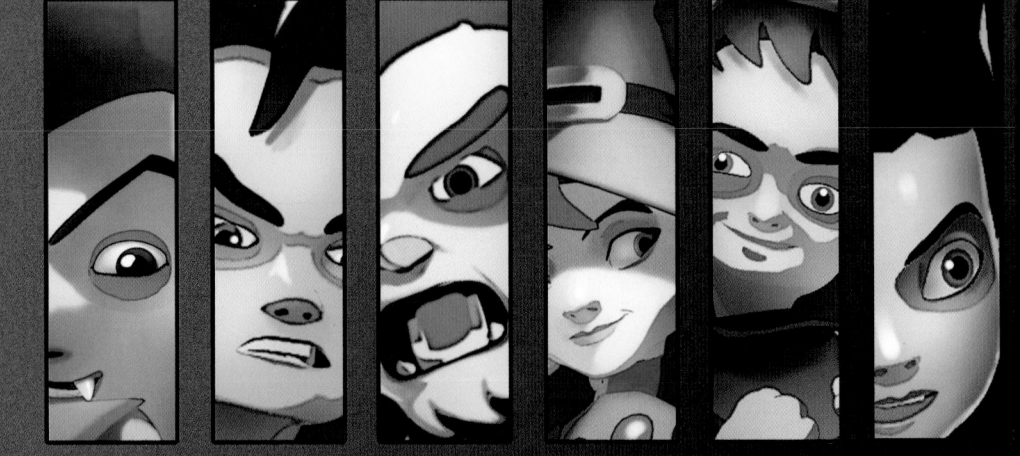

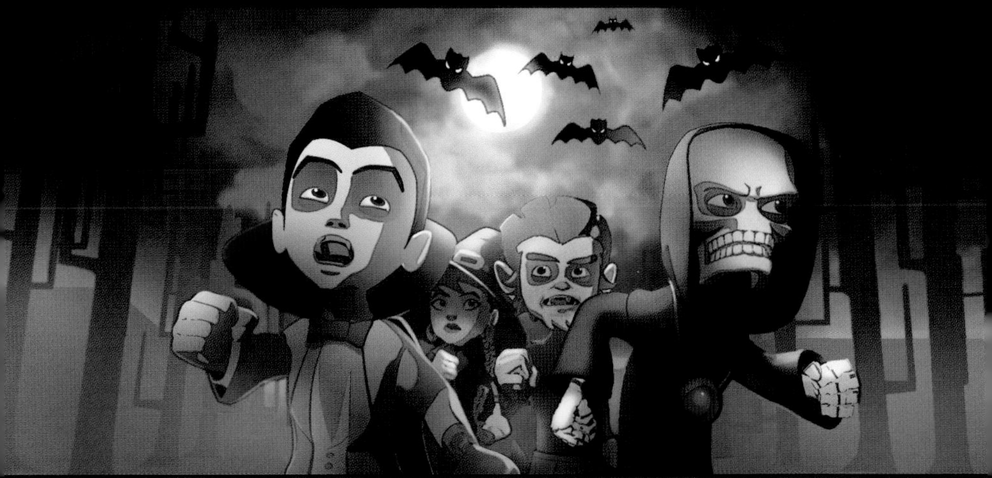

o take on terrifying teachers and homework horrors,
hey formed the most fearsome friendship on Earth . . .

Mighty Mighty MONSTERS

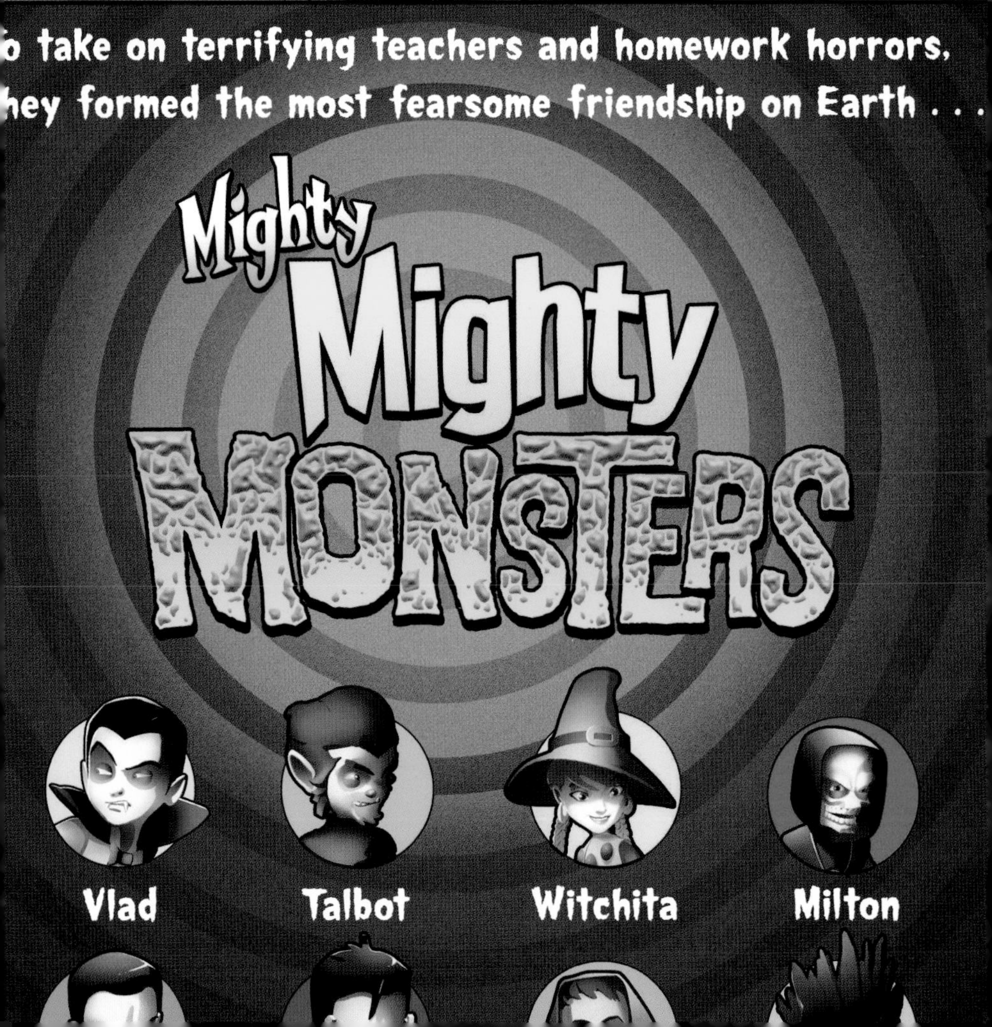
Vlad
Talbot
Witchita
Milton

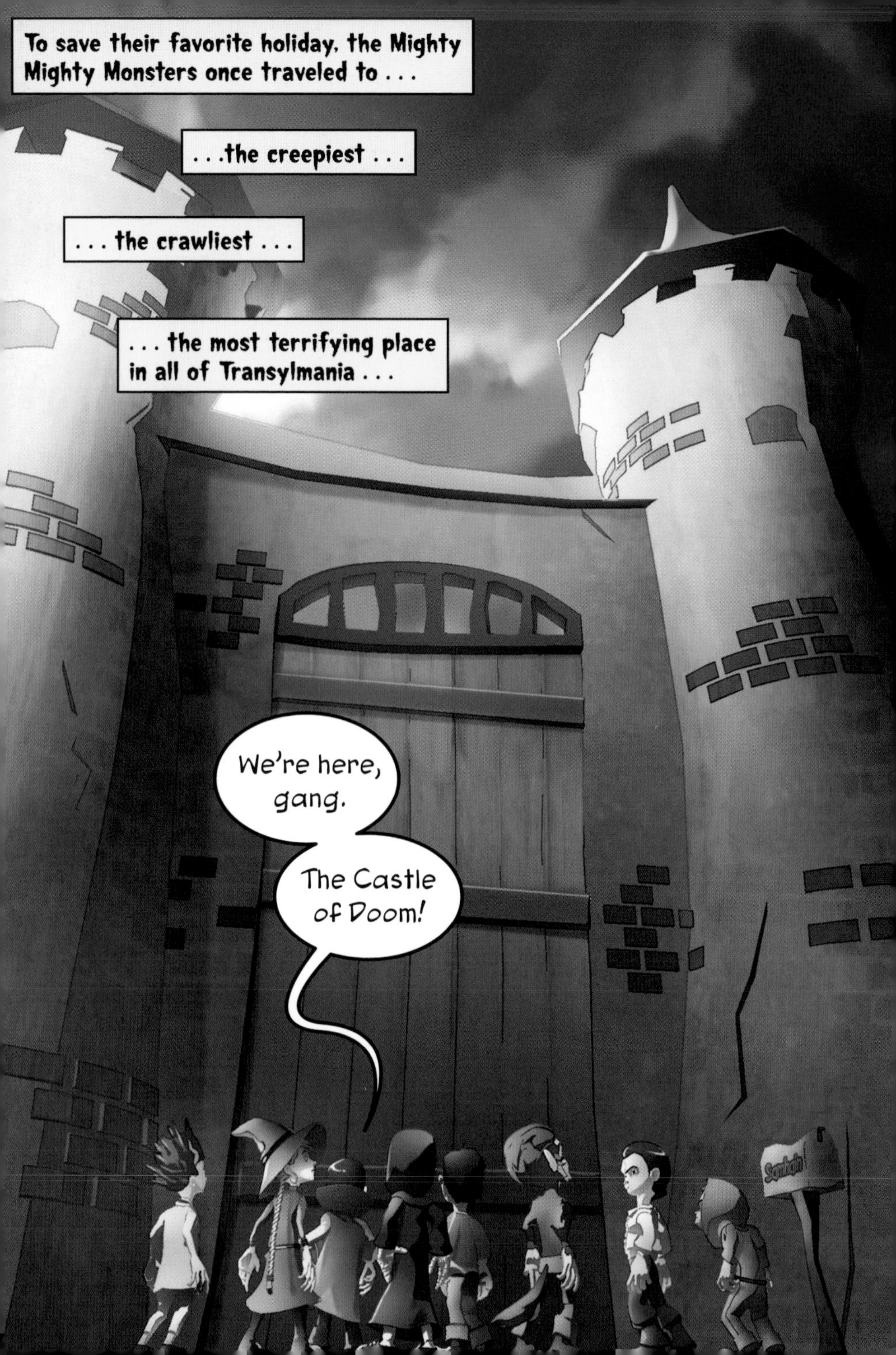
To save their favorite holiday, the Mighty Mighty Monsters once traveled to . . .
. . .the creepiest . . .
. . . the crawliest . . .
. . . the most terrifying place in all of Transylmania . . .
We're here, gang.
The Castle of Doom!
Samhain

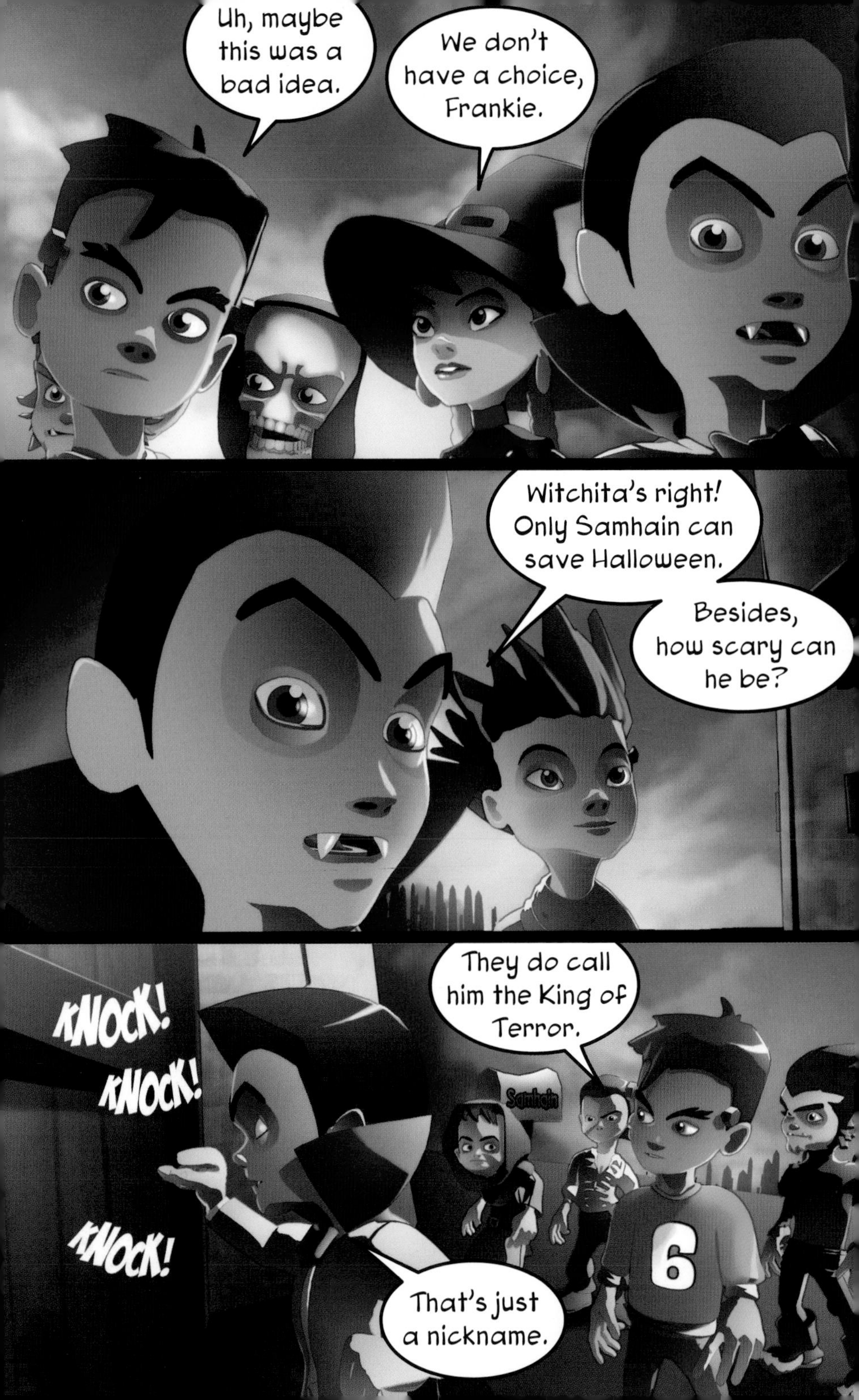
Uh, maybe this was a bad idea.
We don't have a choice, Frankie.
Witchita's right! Only Samhain can save Halloween.
Besides, how scary can he be?
They do call him the King of Terror.
Samhain
KNOCK!
KNOCK!
KNOCK!
That's just a nickname.

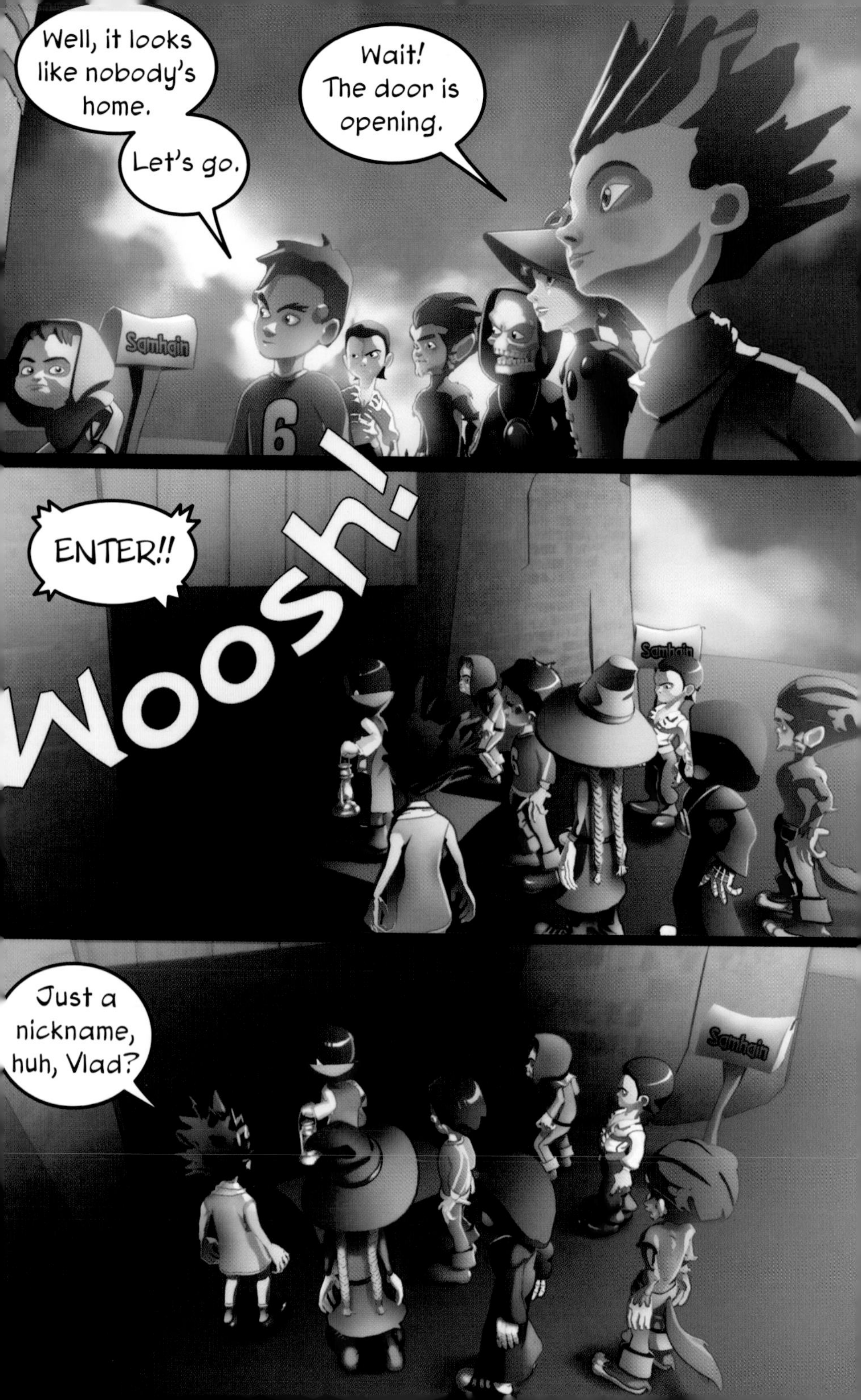
Well, it looks like nobody's home.
Let's go.
Wait! The door is opening.
Samhain
ENTER!!
Woosh!
Samhain
Just a nickname, huh, Vlad?
Samhain

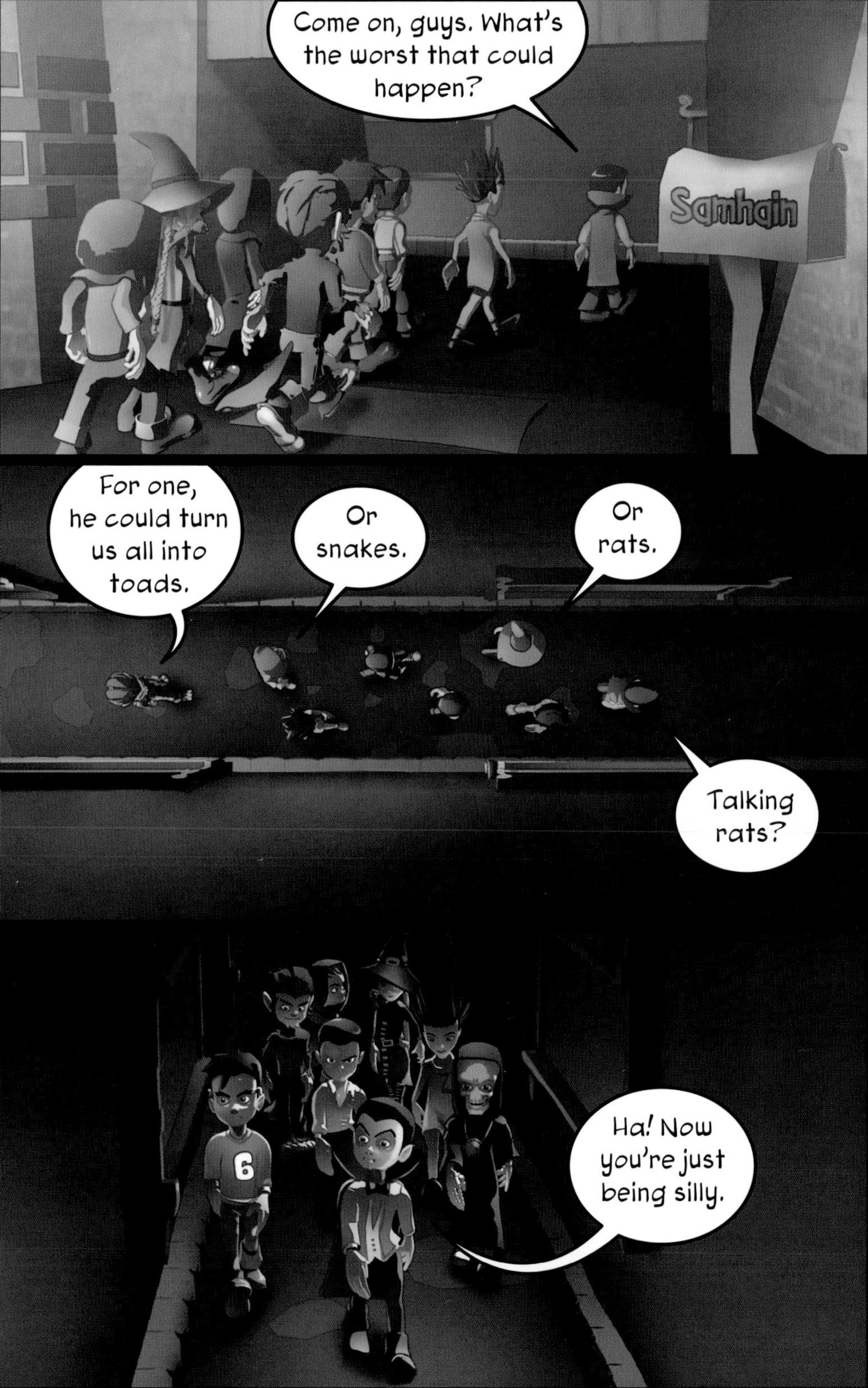
Come on, guys. What's the worst that could happen?
Samhain
For one, he could turn us all into toads.
Or snakes.
Or rats.
Talking rats?
6
Ha! Now you're just being silly.

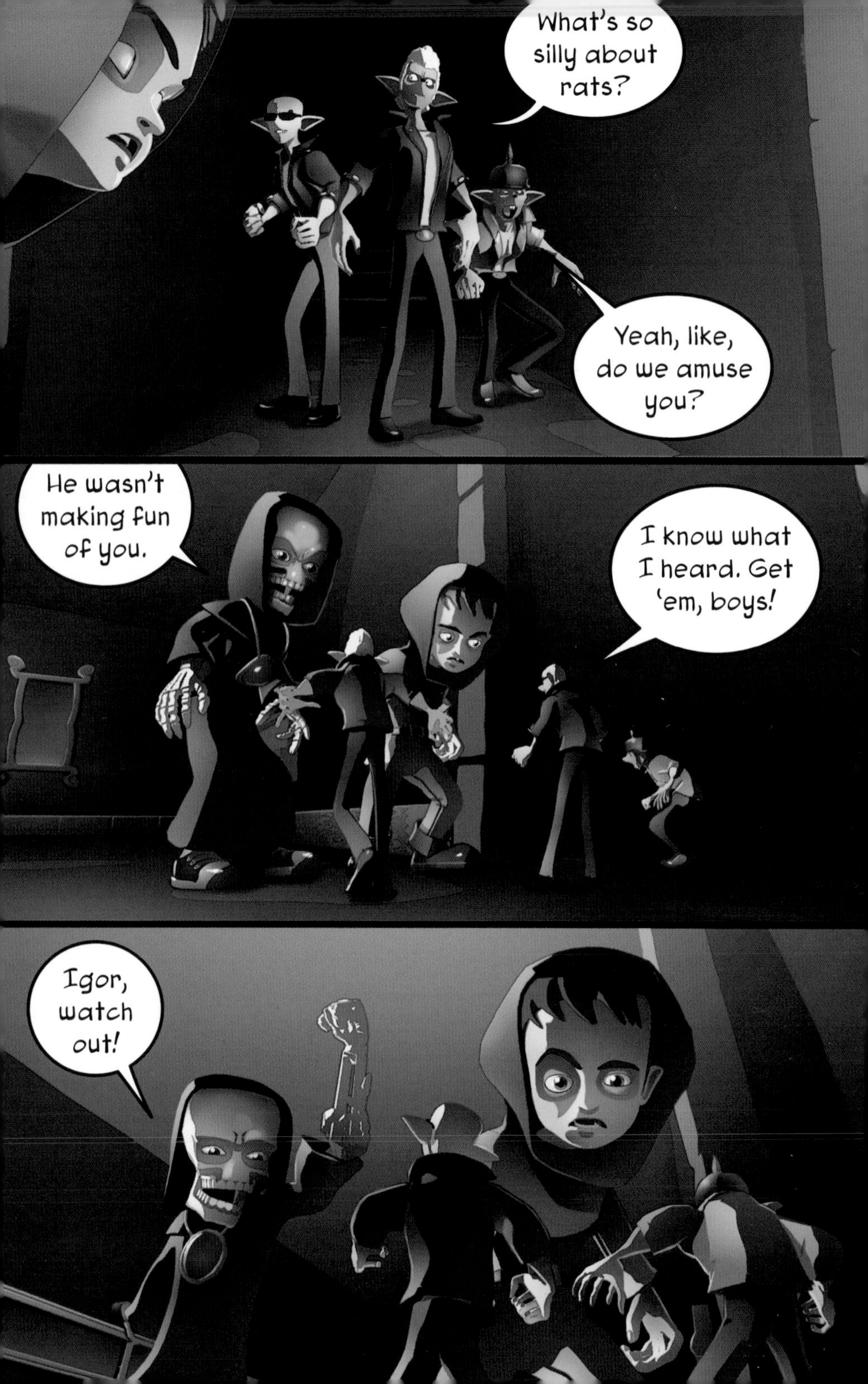
What's so silly about rats?
Yeah, like, do we amuse you?
He wasn't making fun of you.
I know what I heard. Get 'em, boys!
Igor, watch out!

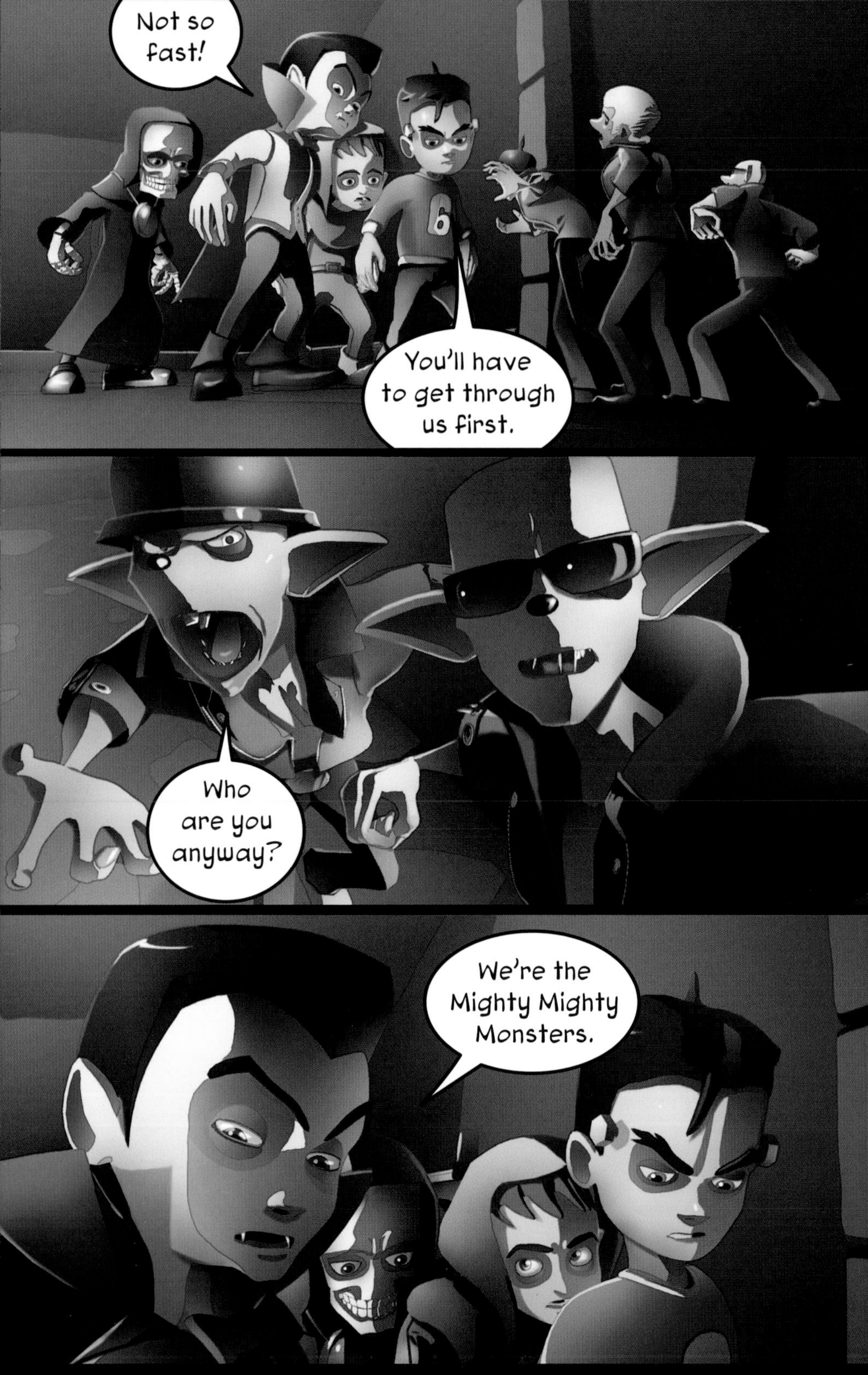
Not so fast!
You'll have to get through us first.
Who are you anyway?
We're the Mighty Mighty Monsters.

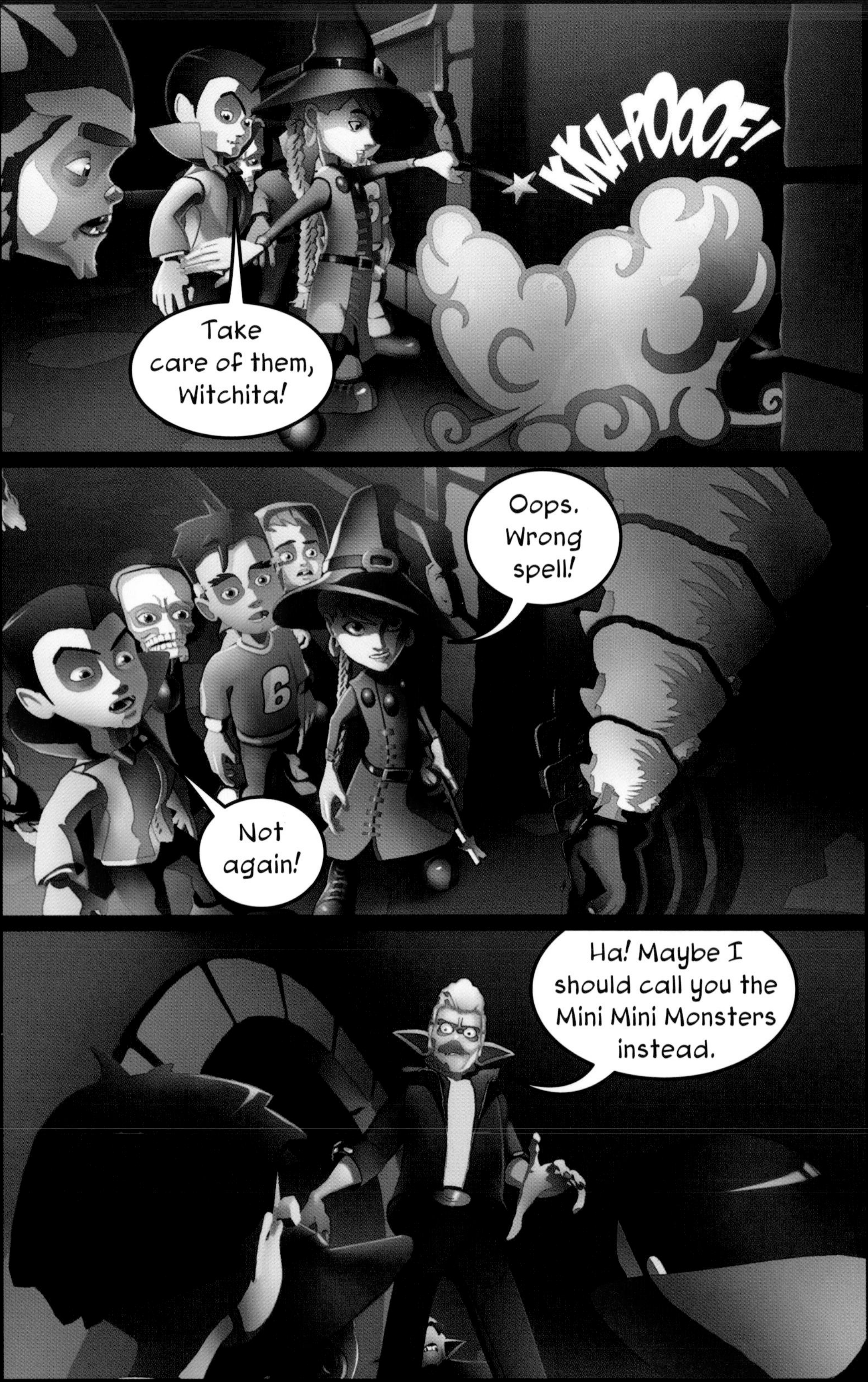
Take care of them, Witchita!
KKA-POOOF!
Oops. Wrong spell!
Not again!
Ha! Maybe I should call you the Mini Mini Monsters instead.

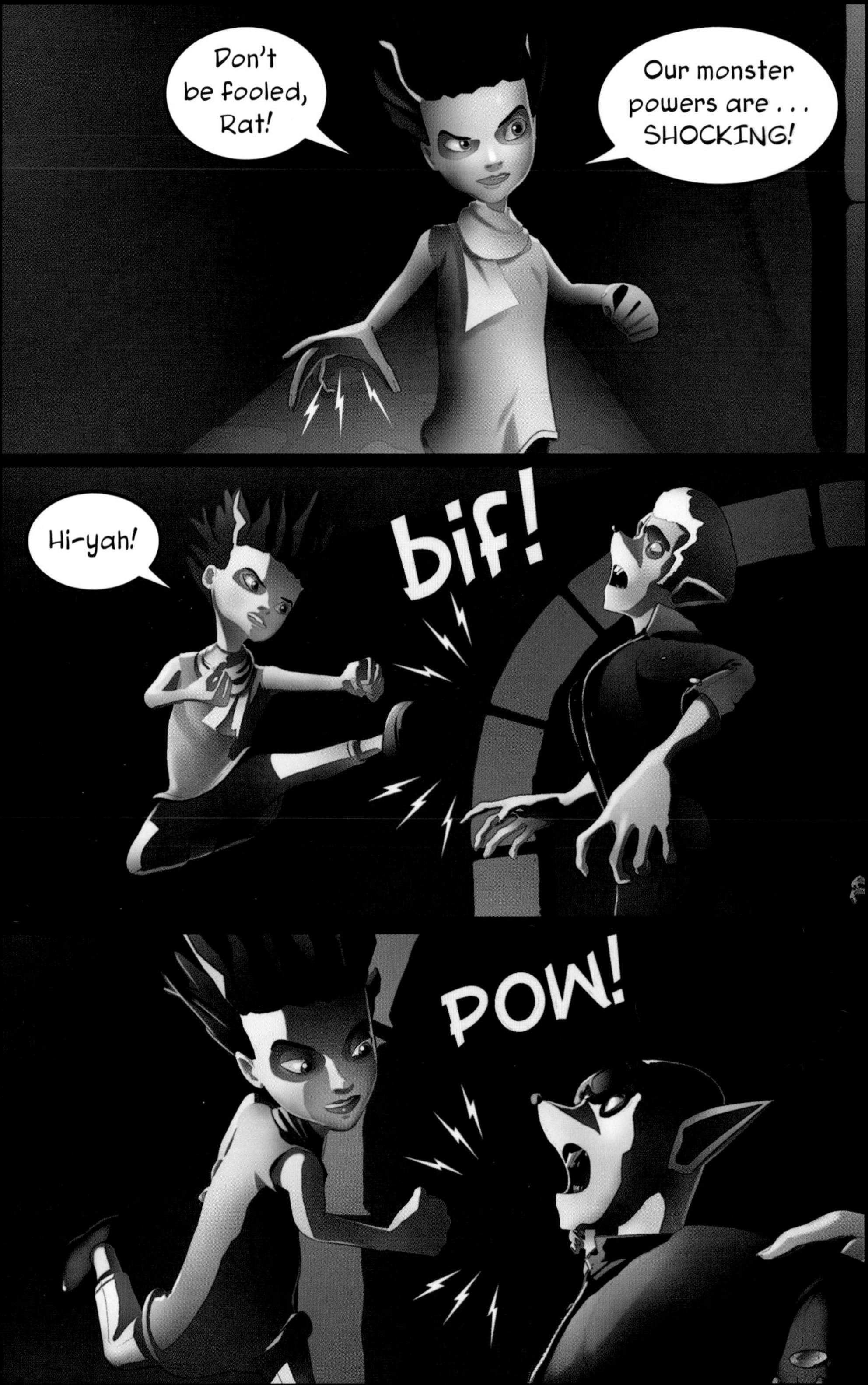
Don't be fooled, Rat!
Our monster powers are . . . SHOCKING!
Hi-yah!
bif!
POW!

POW!
thud
Wow, Mary, that was —
Electrifying?
Totally.

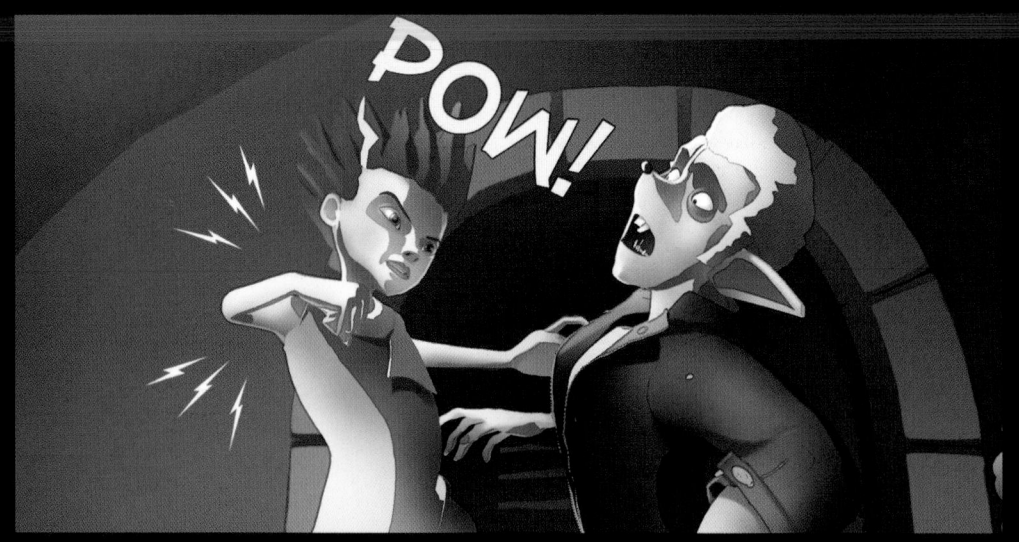

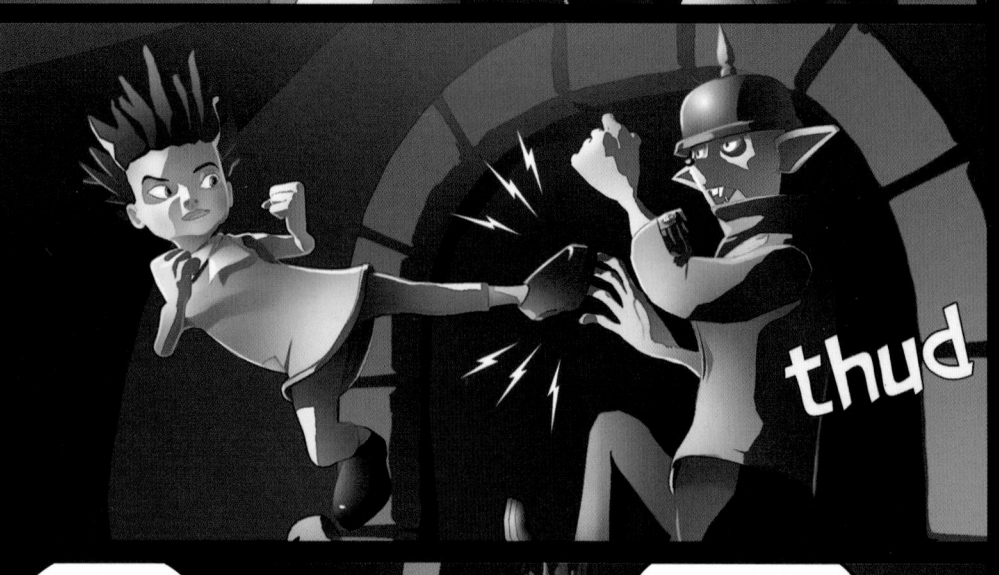

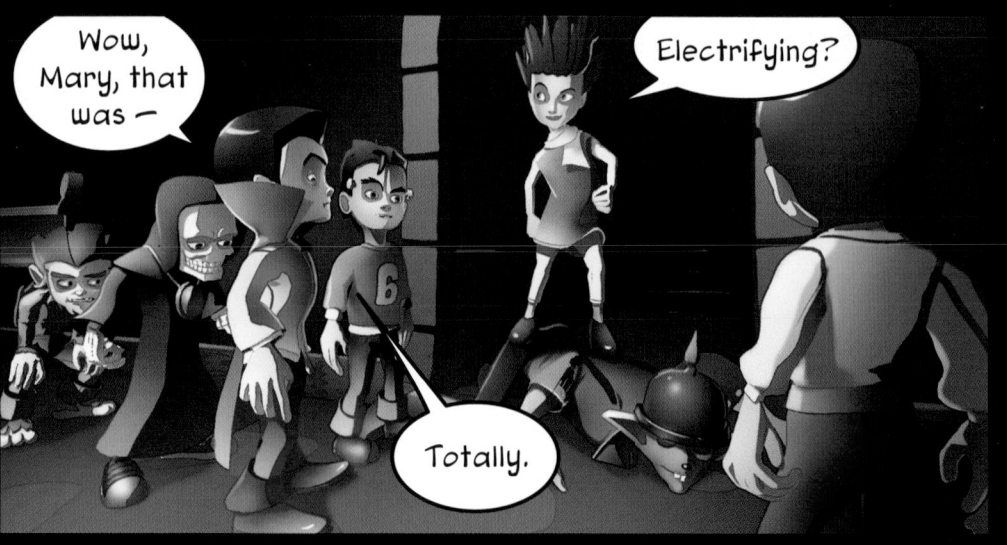

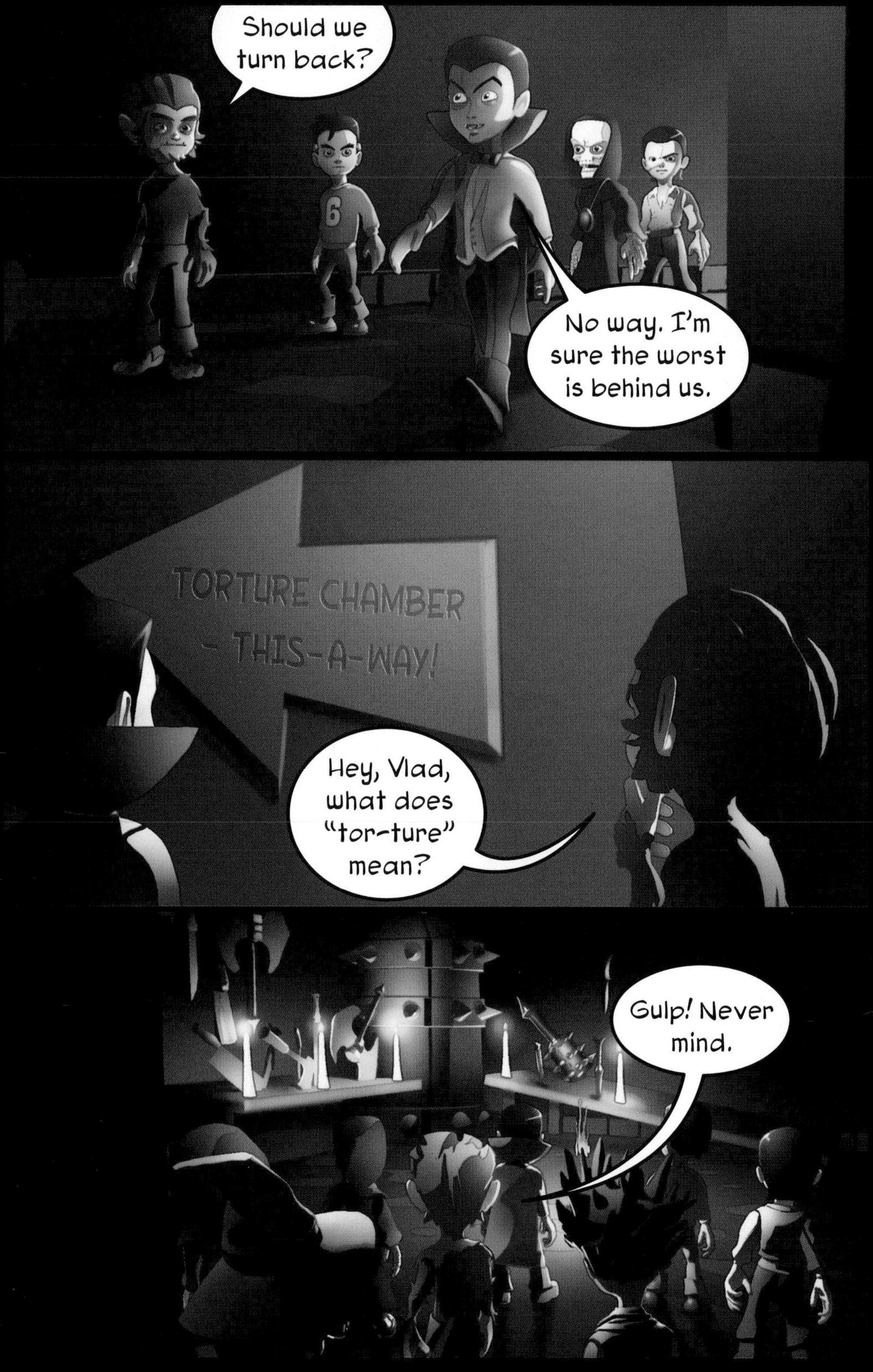
Should we turn back?
No way. I'm sure the worst is behind us.
TORTURE CHAMBER – THIS-A-WAY!
Hey, Vlad, what does "tor-ture" mean?
Gulp! Never mind.

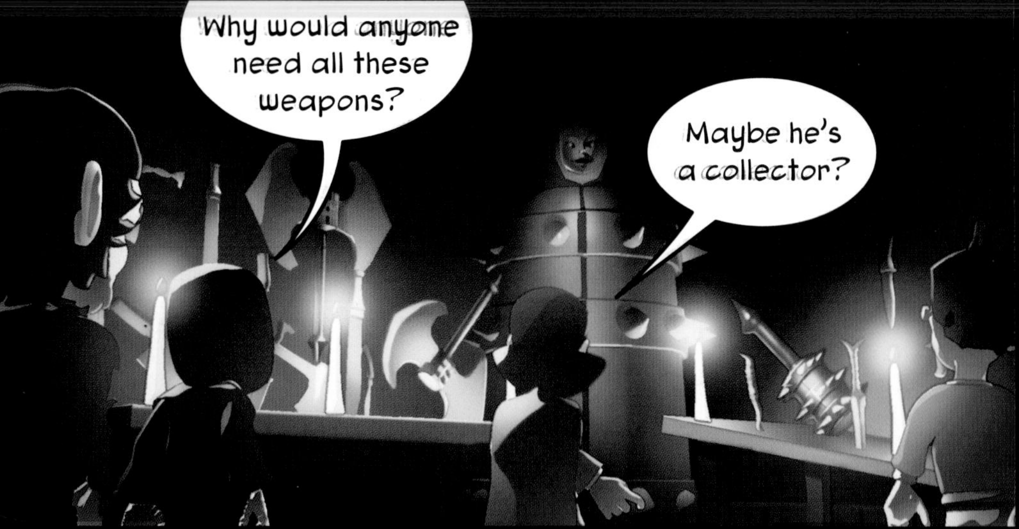
Why would anyone need all these weapons?
Maybe he's a collector?

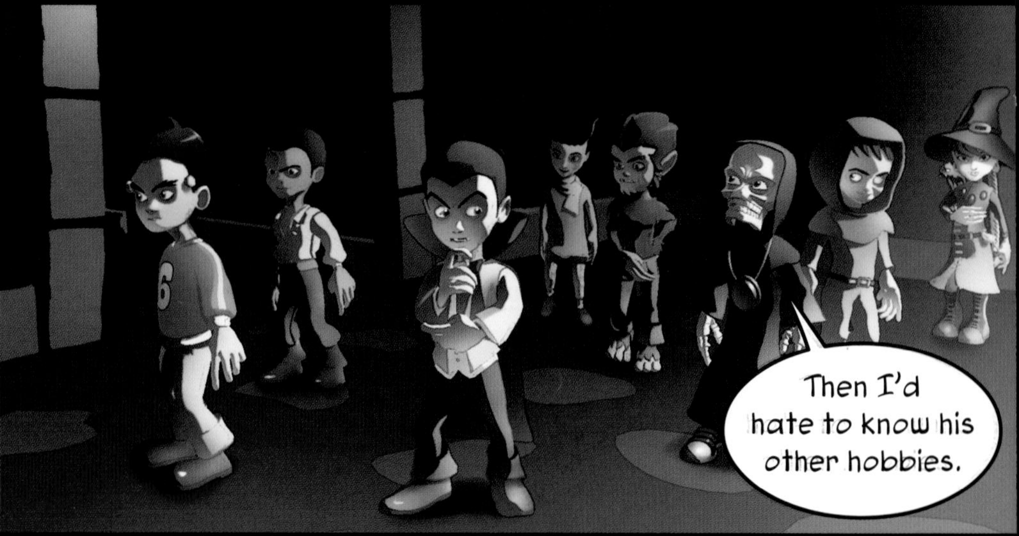
Then I'd hate to know his other hobbies.

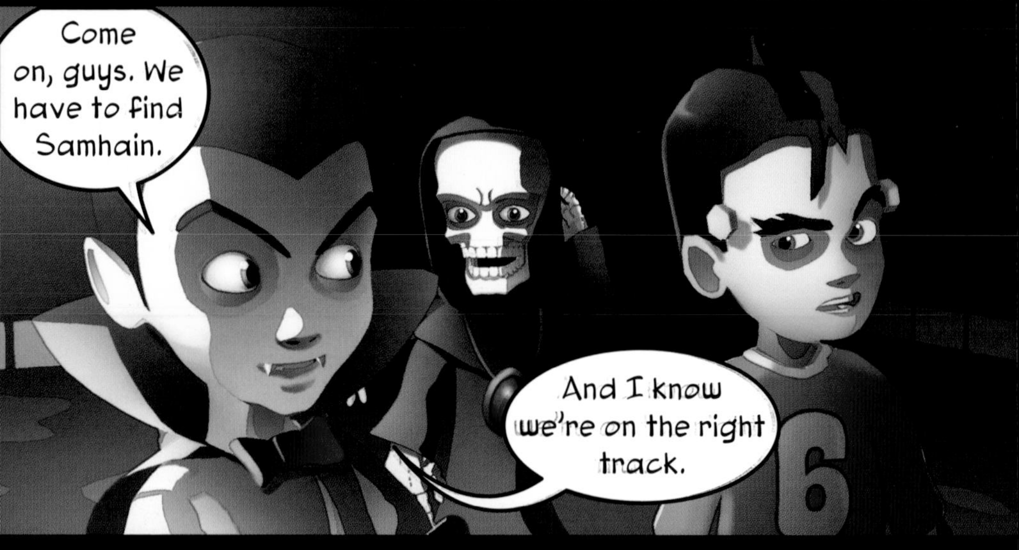
Come on, guys. We have to find Samhain.
And I know we're on the right track.

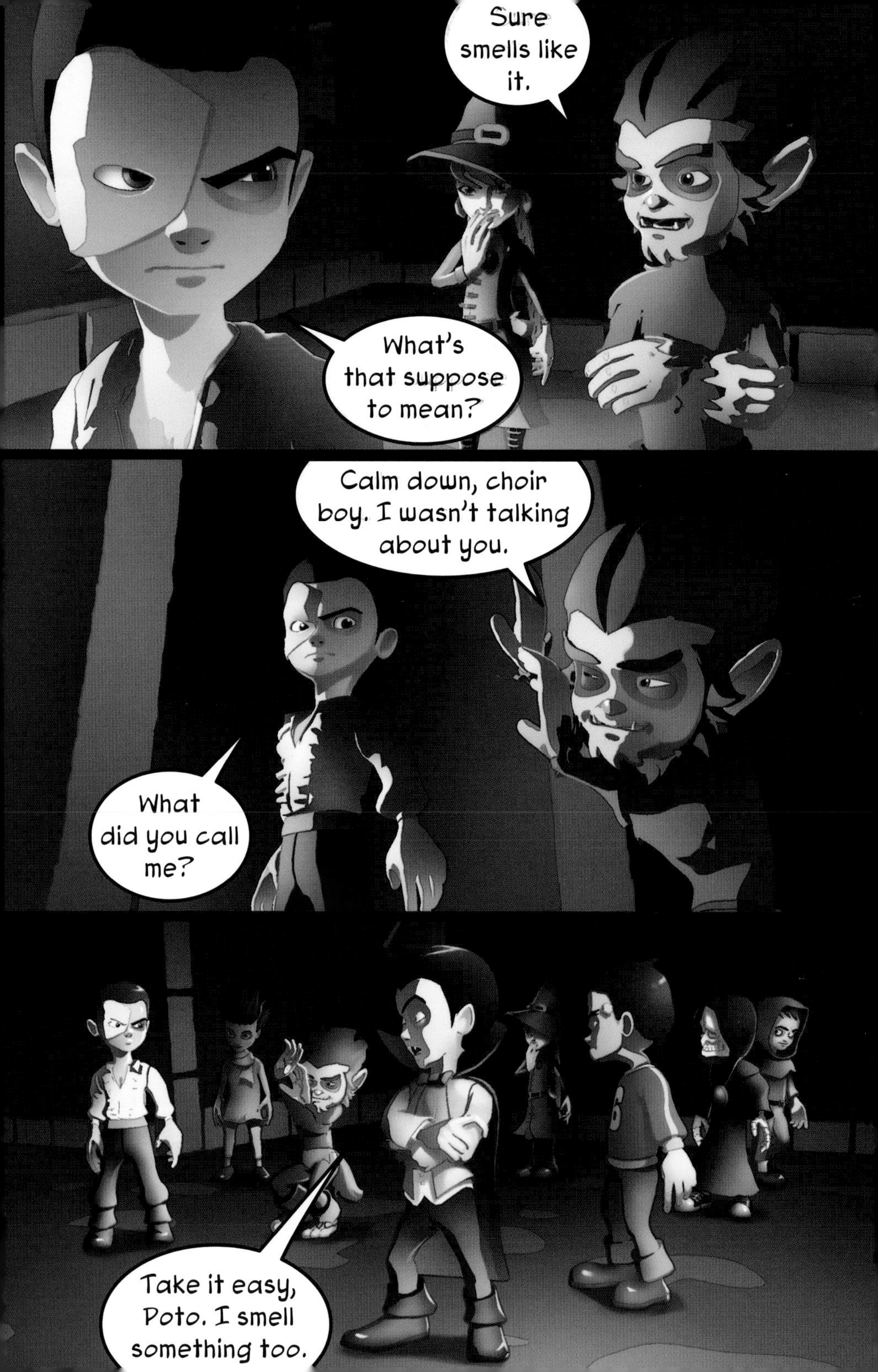
Sure smells like it.
What's that suppose to mean?
Calm down, choir boy. I wasn't talking about you.
What did you call me?
Take it easy, Poto. I smell something too.

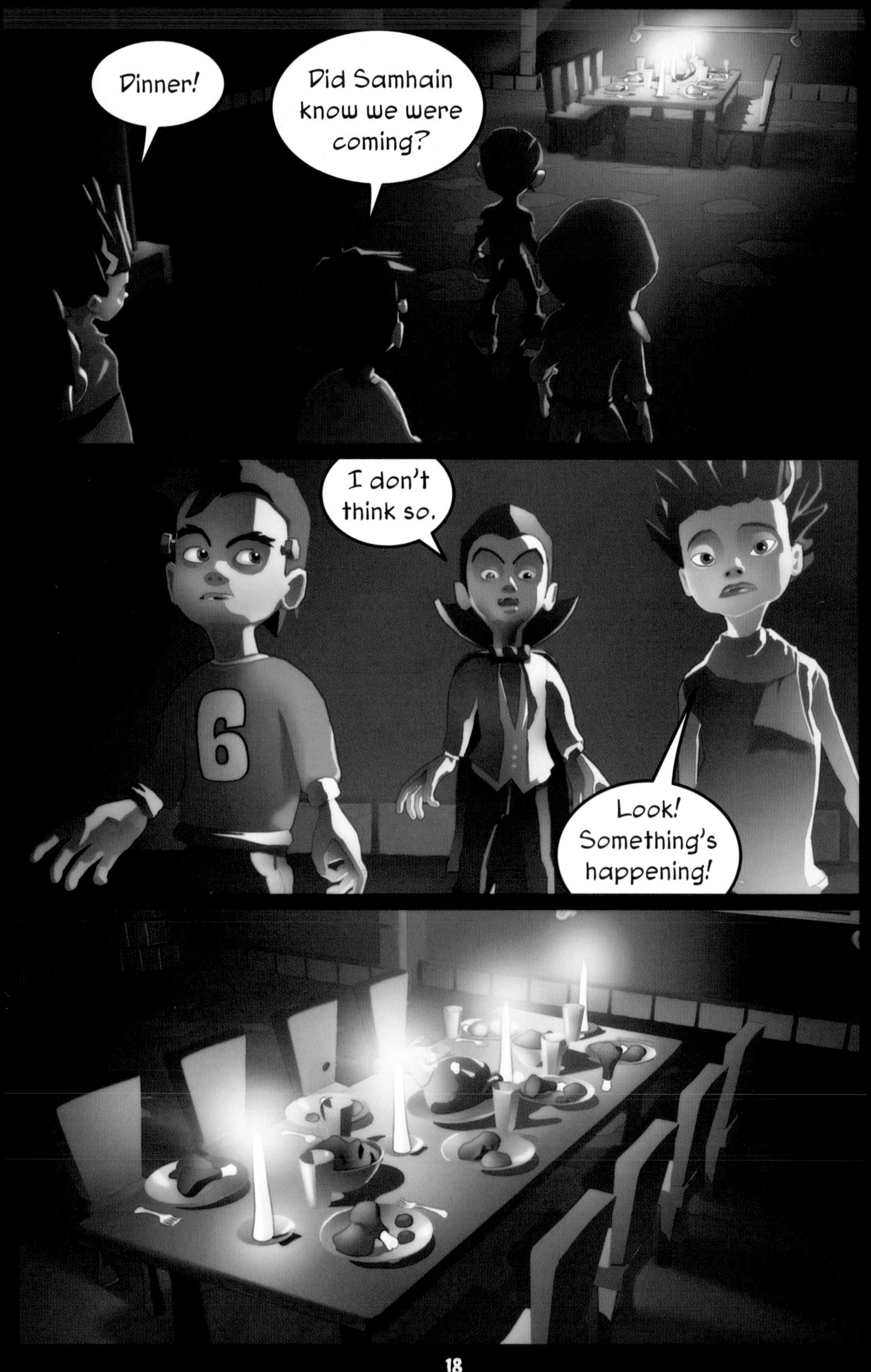
Dinner!
Did Samhain know we were coming?
I don't think so.
Look! Something's happening!
6

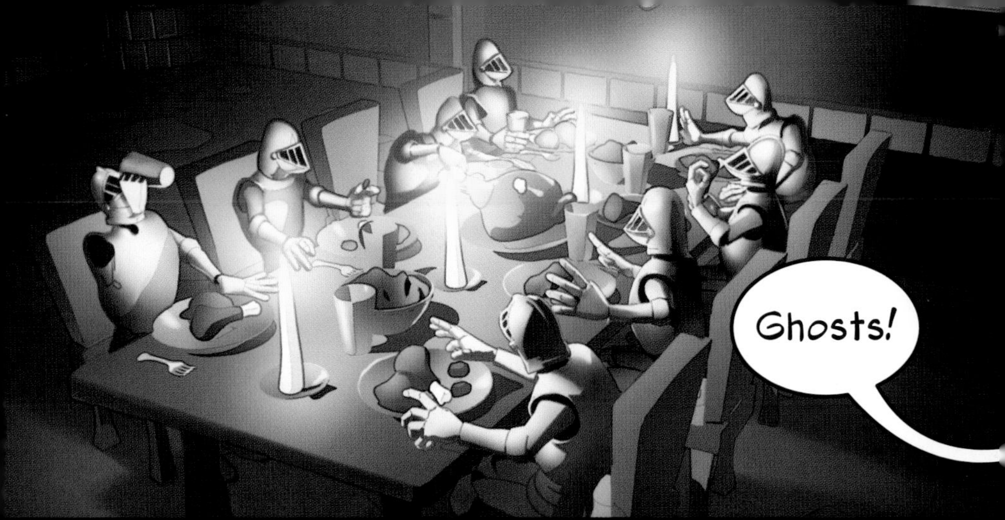
Ghosts!

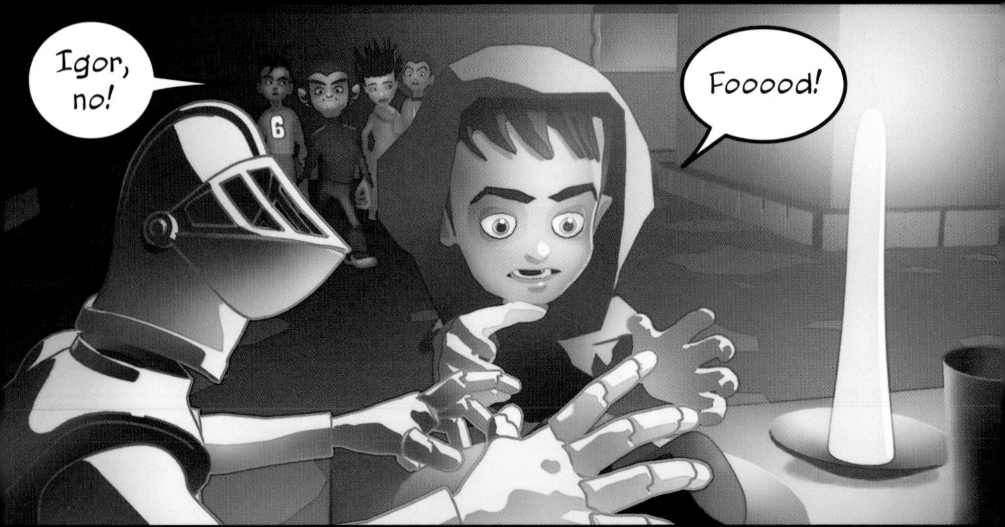
Igor, no!
Fooood!

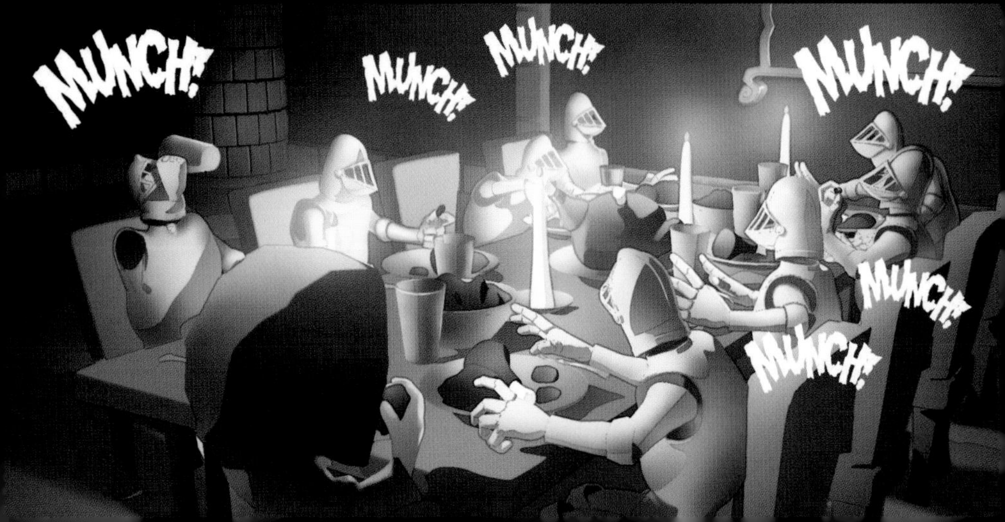
MUNCH!
MUNCH!
MUNCH!
MUNCH!
MUNCH!
MUNCH!

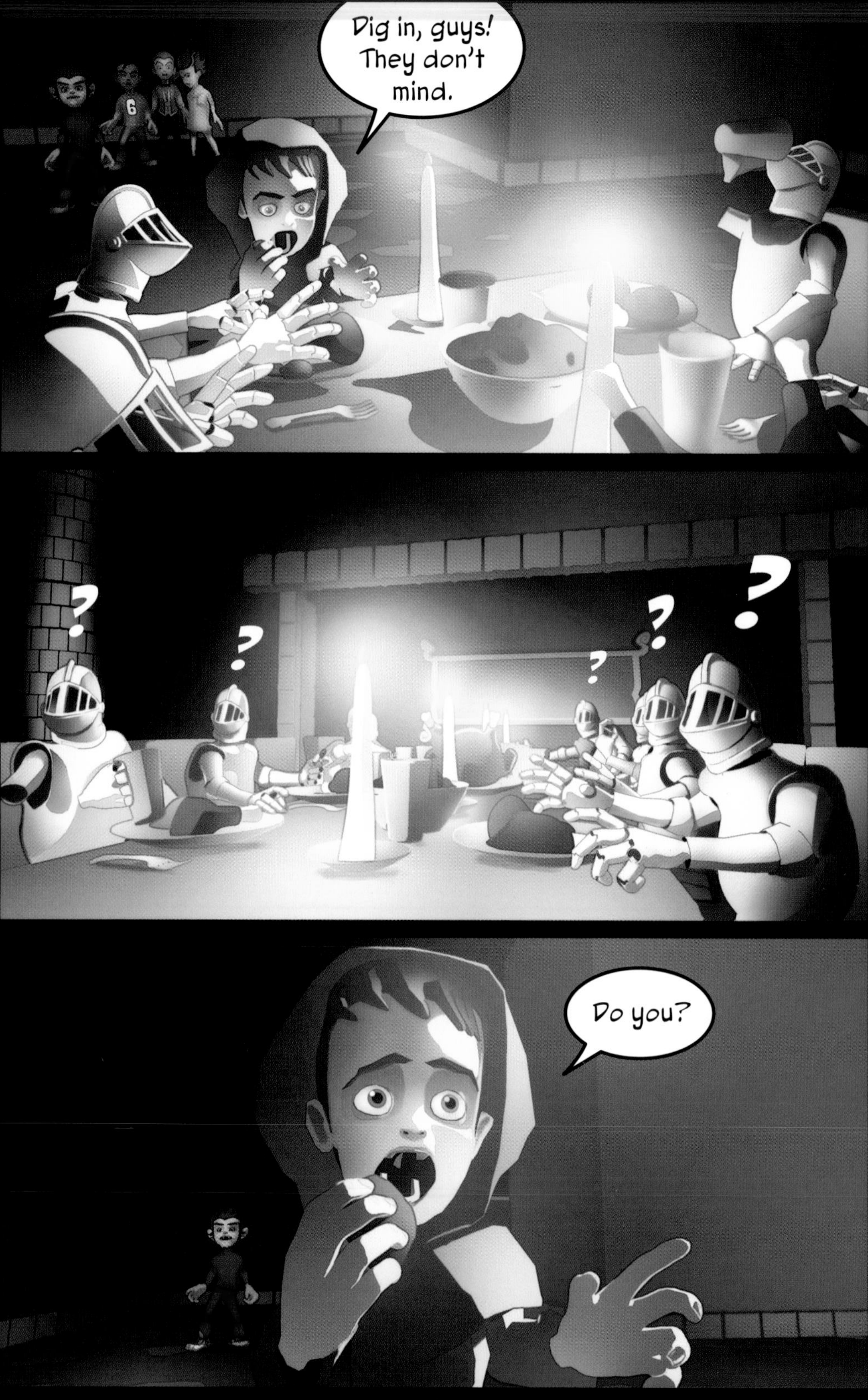
Dig in, guys! They don't mind.
? ? ? ? ?
Do you?

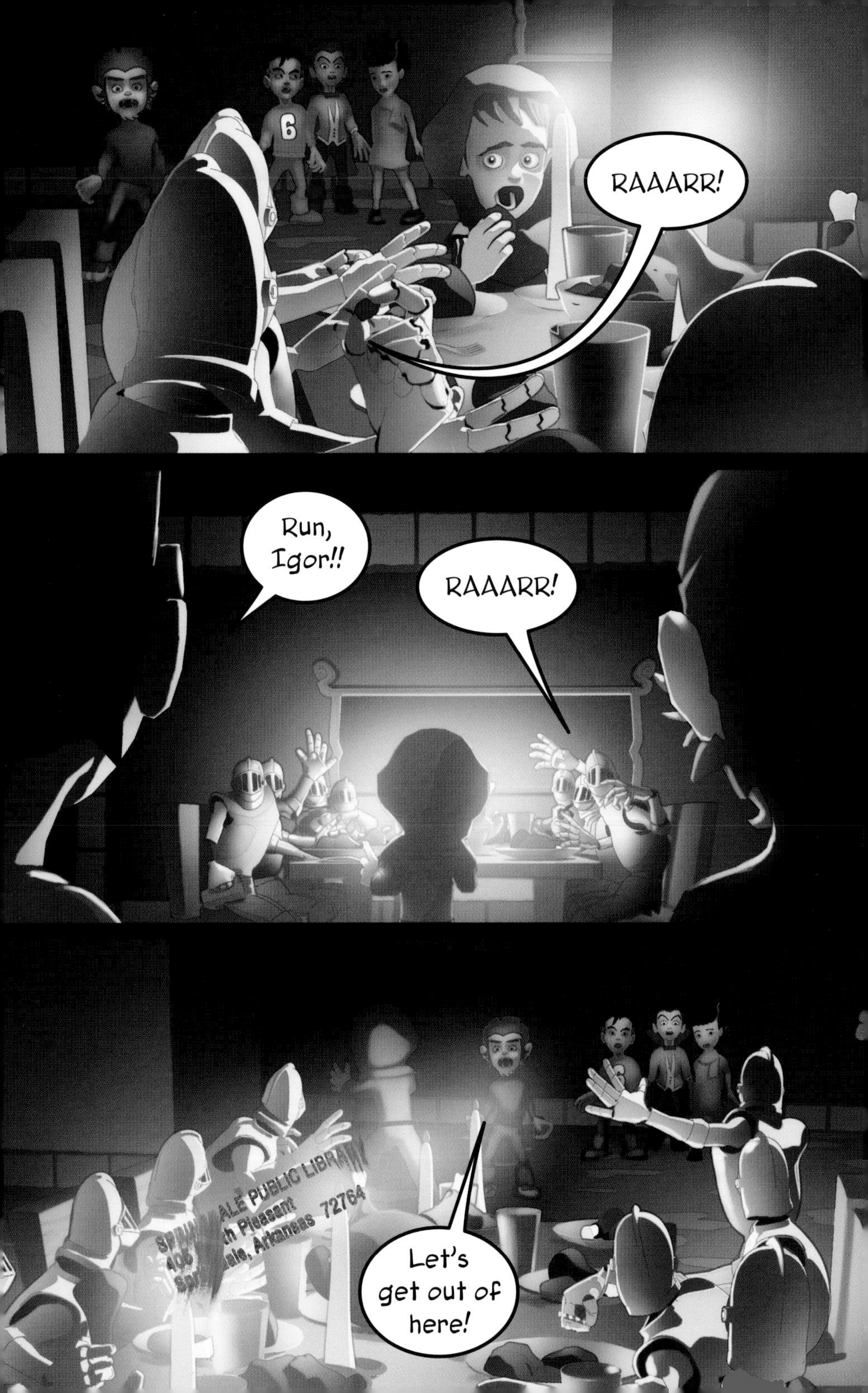
RAAARR!
Run, Igor!!
RAAARR!
Let's get out of here!

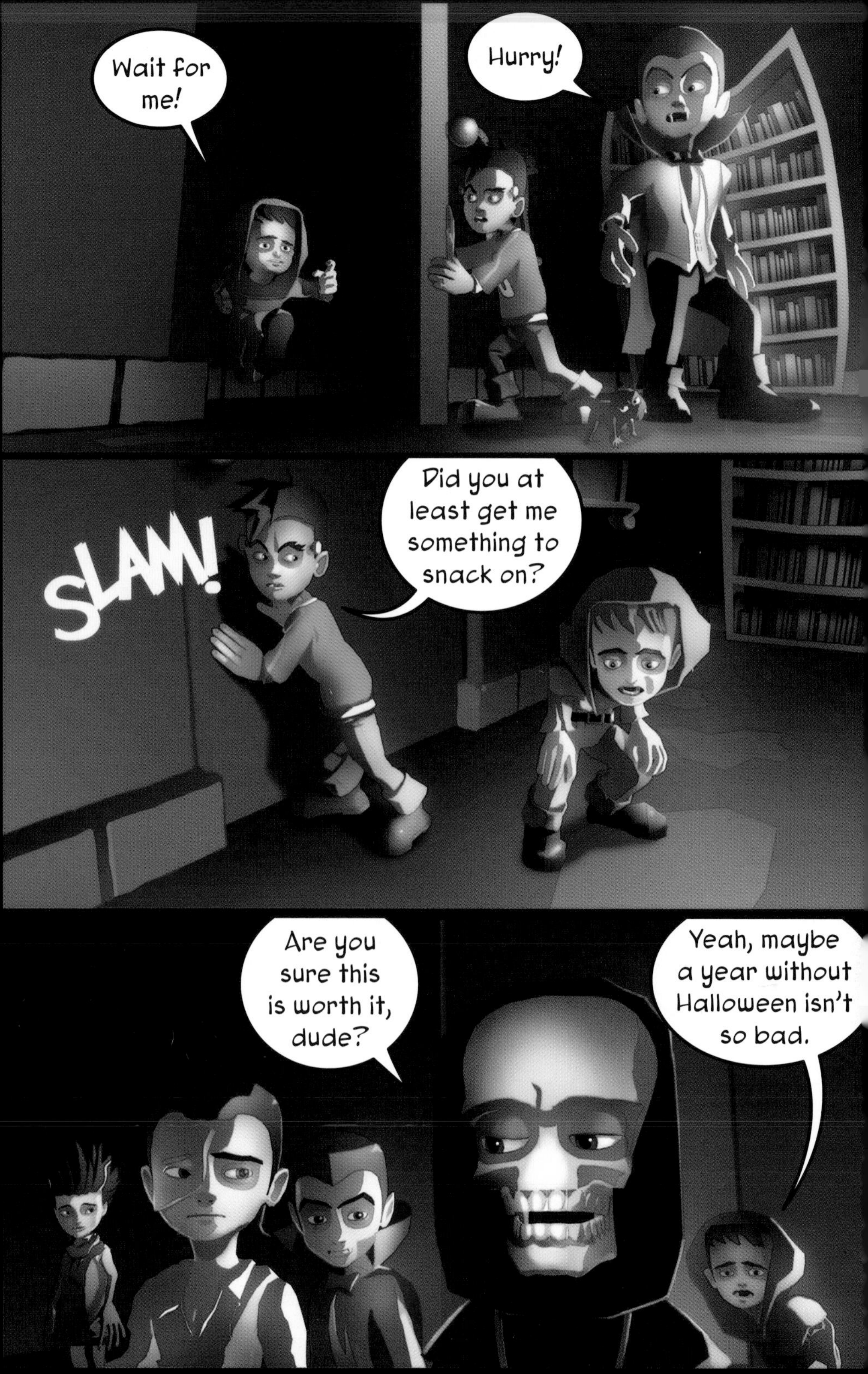
Wait for me!
Hurry!
SLAM!
Did you at least get me something to snack on?
Are you sure this is worth it, dude?
Yeah, maybe a year without Halloween isn't so bad.

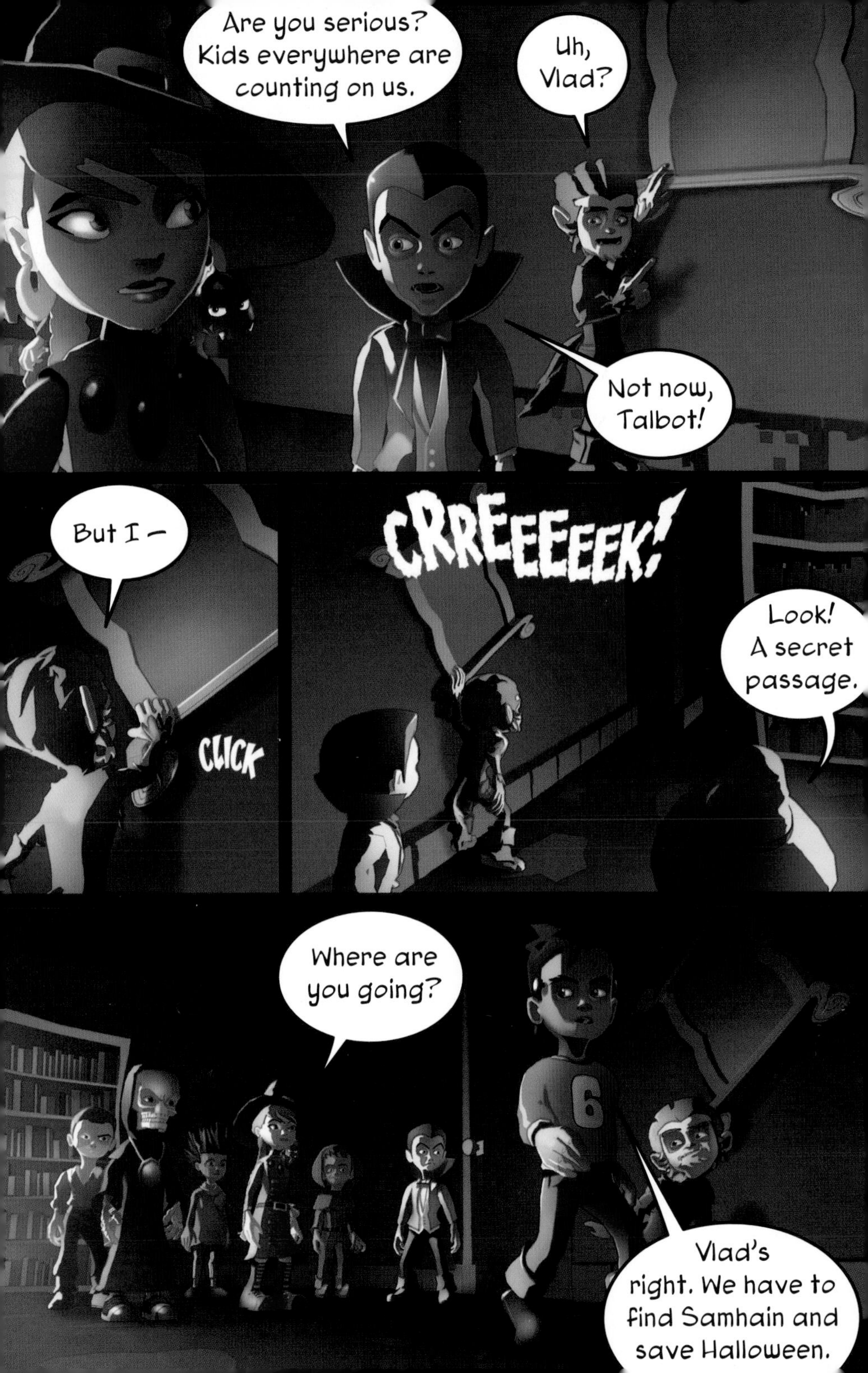
Are you serious? Kids everywhere are counting on us.
Uh, Vlad?
Not now, Talbot!
But I —
CLICK
CRREEEEEK!
Look! A secret passage.
Where are you going?
Vlad's right. We have to find Samhain and save Halloween.

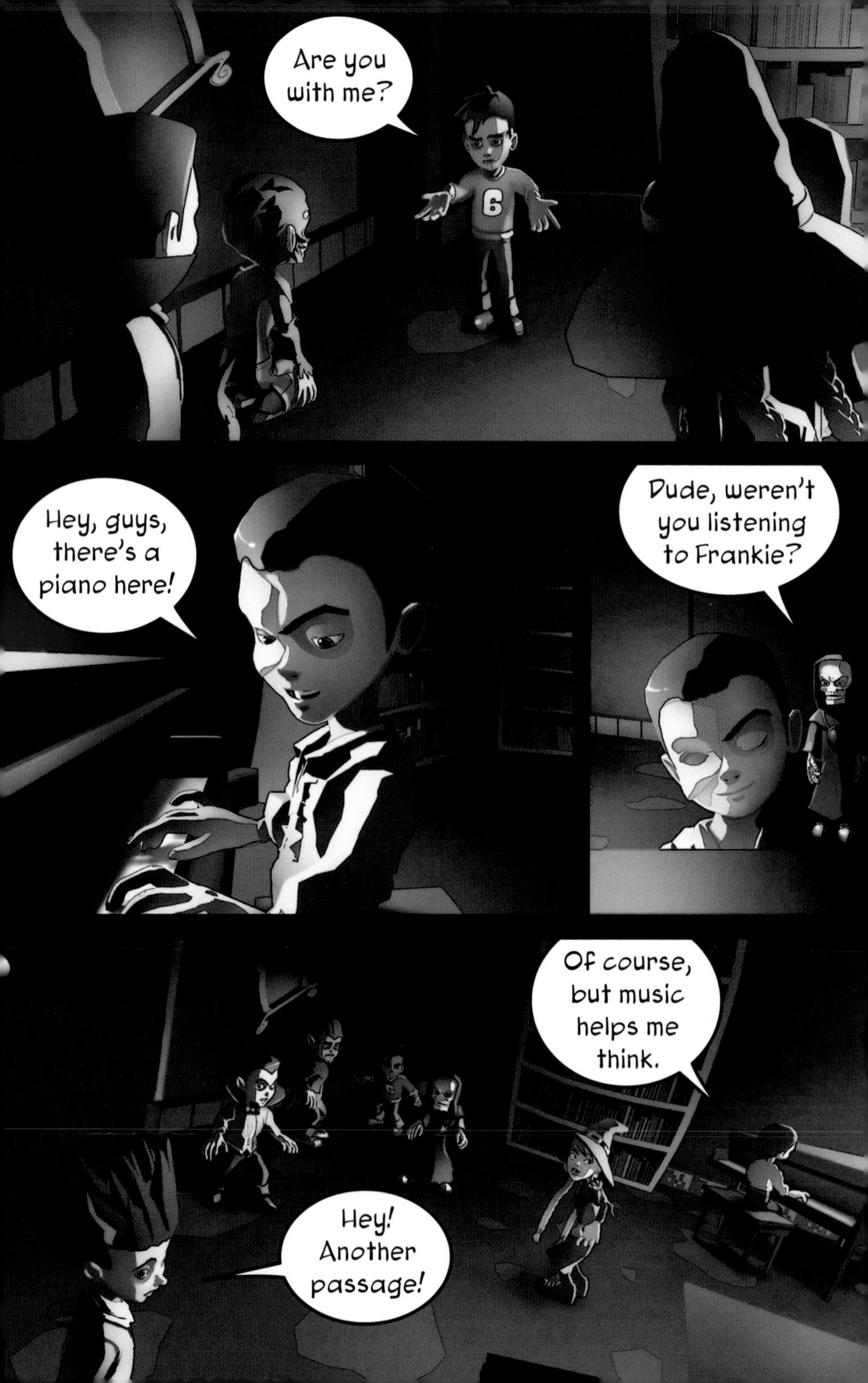
Are you with me?
Hey, guys, there's a piano here!
Dude, weren't you listening to Frankie?
Of course, but music helps me think.
Hey! Another passage!

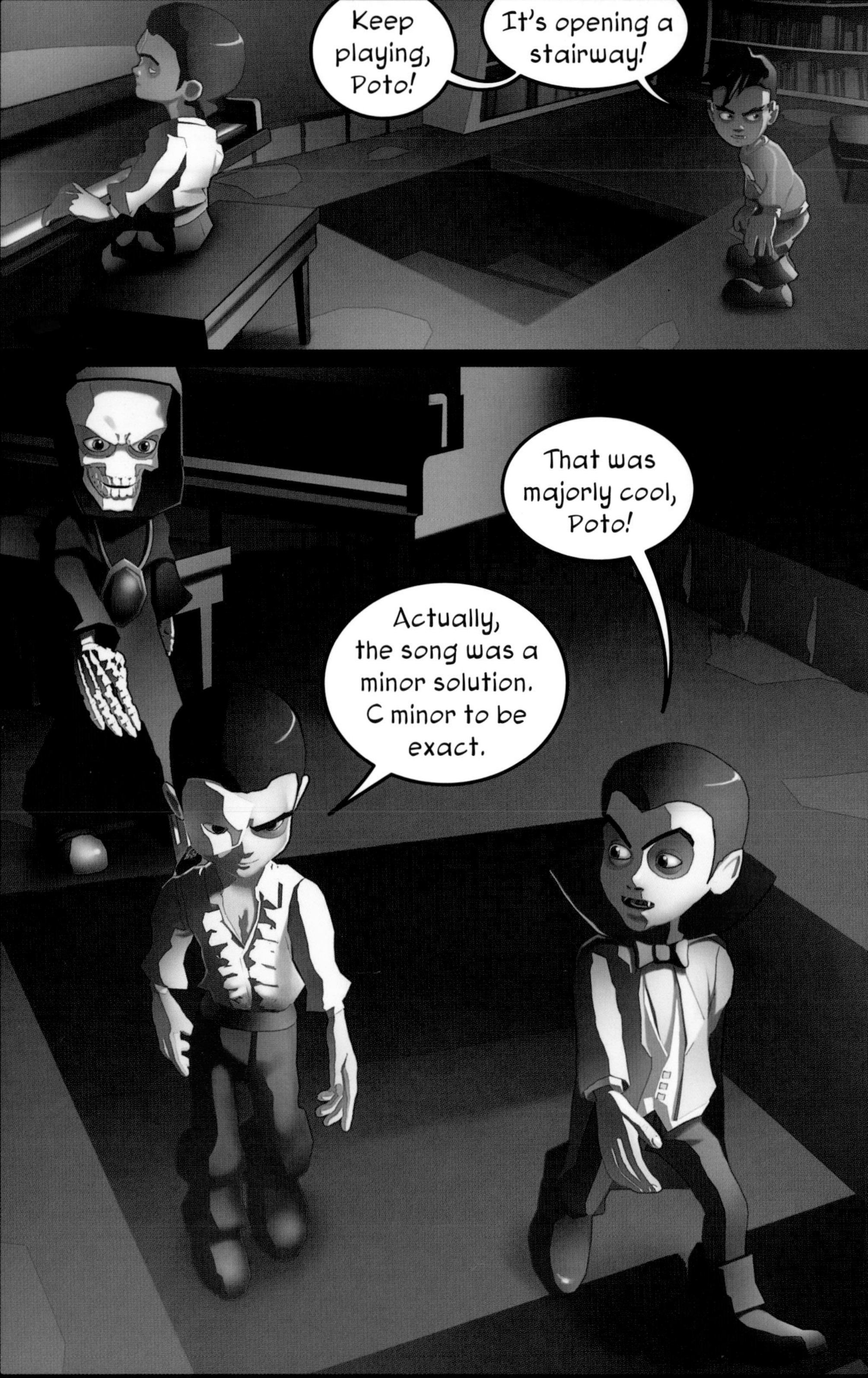
Keep playing, Poto!
It's opening a stairway!
That was majorly cool, Poto!
Actually, the song was a minor solution. C minor to be exact.

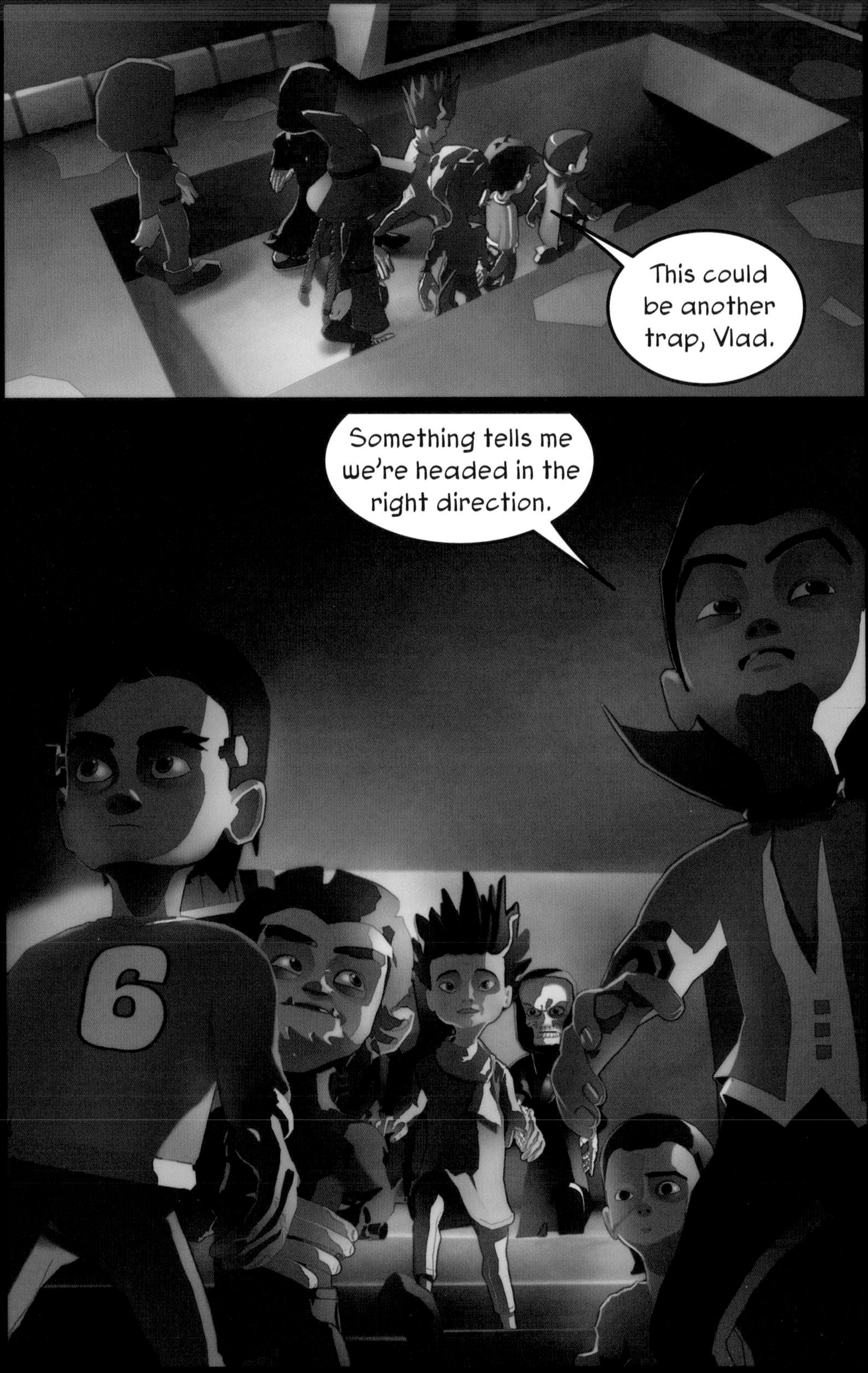
This could be another trap, Vlad.
Something tells me we're headed in the right direction.
6

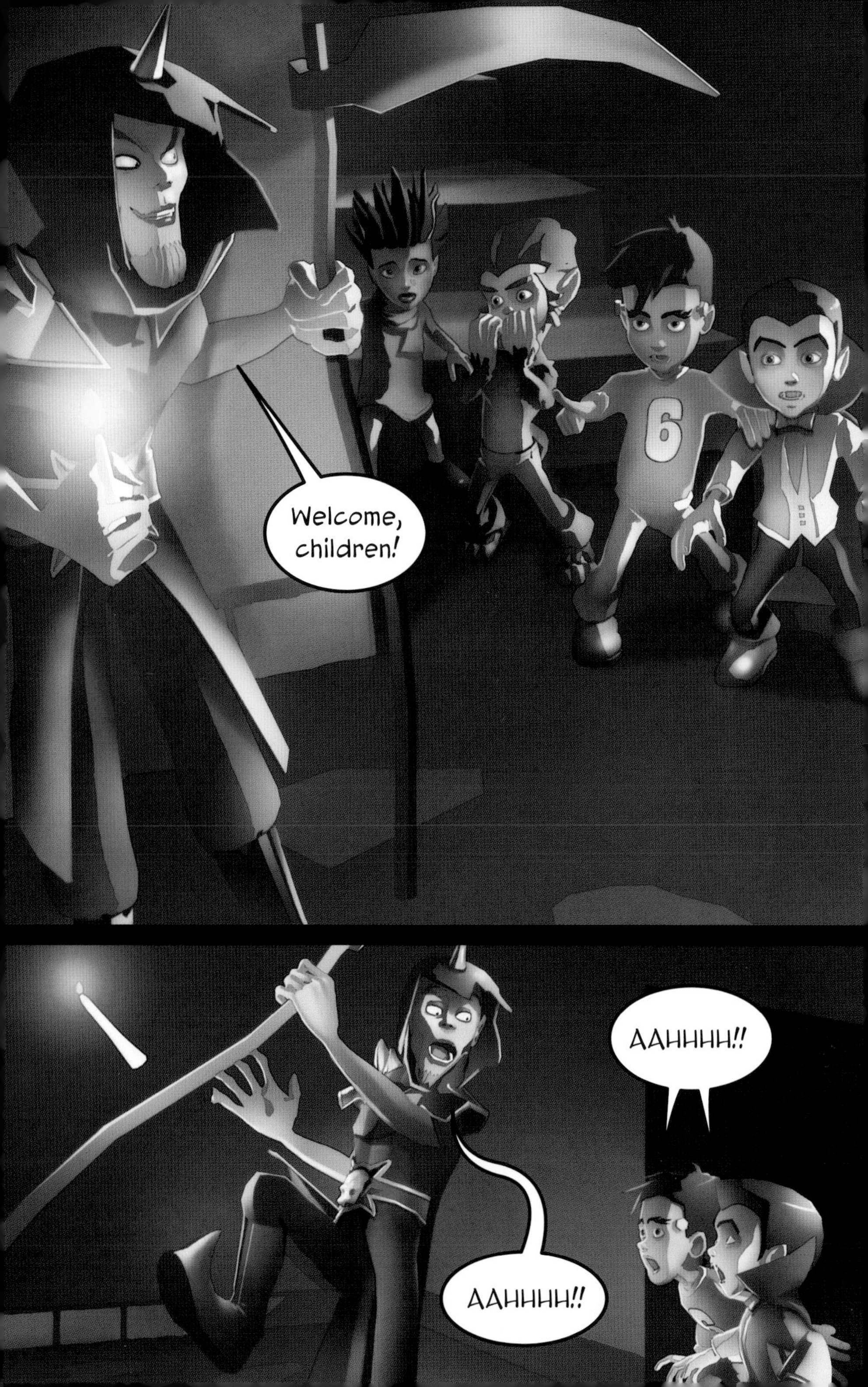
Welcome, children!
AAHHHH!!
AAHHHH!!

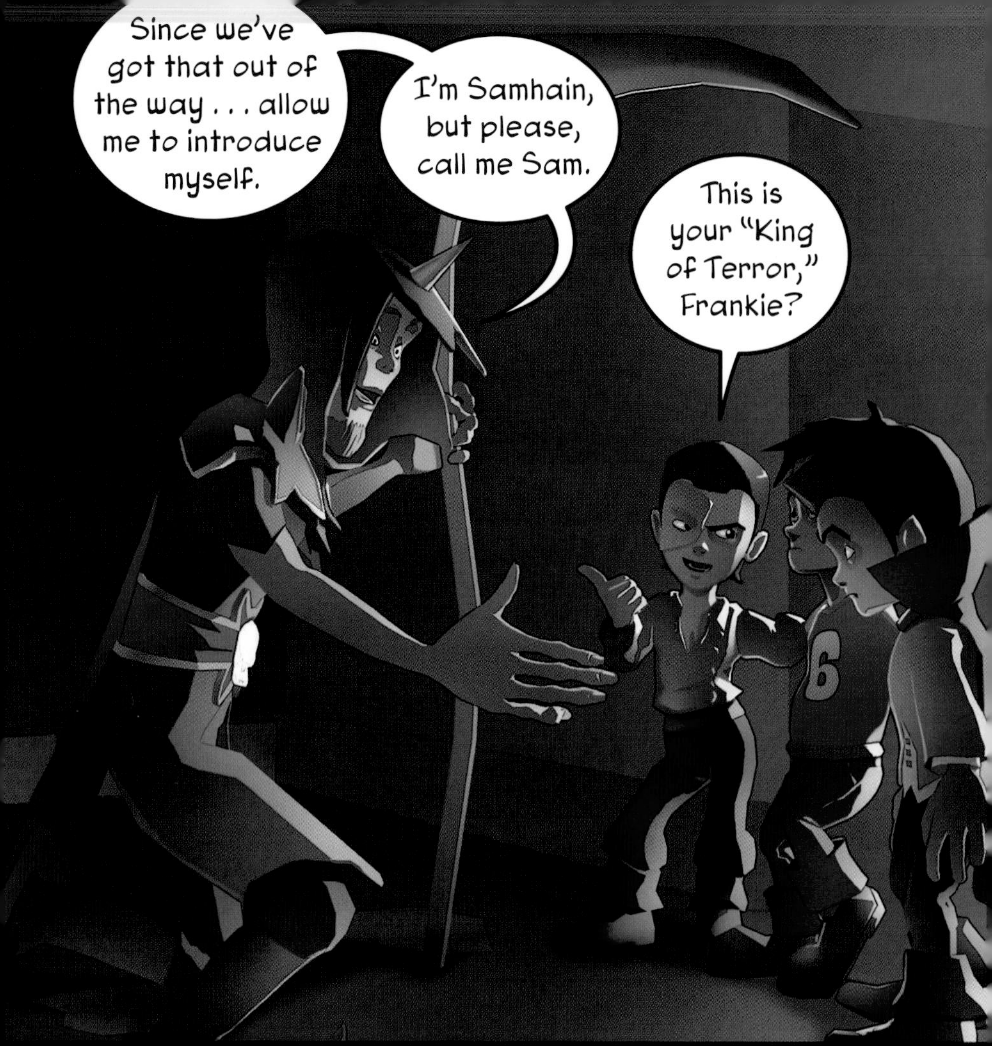

Since we've got that out of the way . . . allow me to introduce myself.
I'm Samhain, but please, call me Sam.
This is your "King of Terror," Frankie?

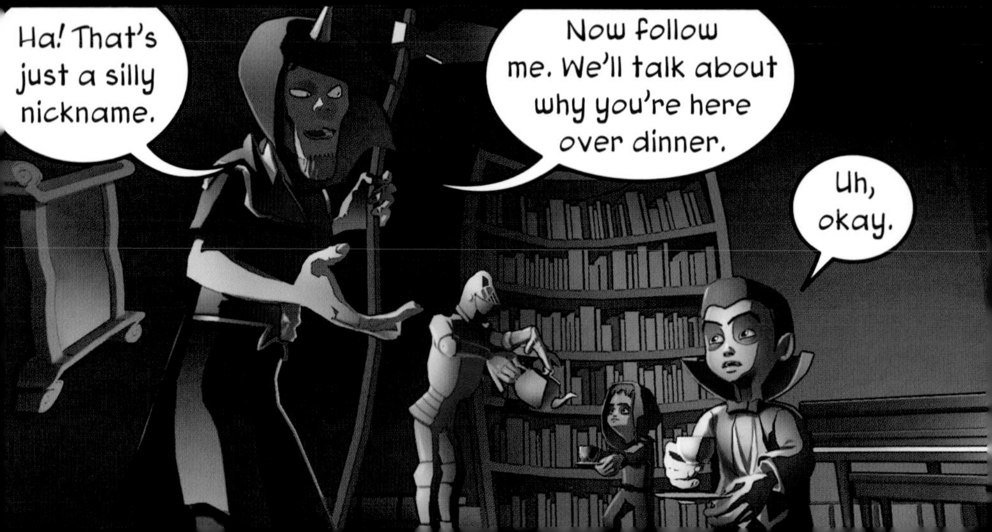

Ha! That's just a silly nickname.
Now follow me. We'll talk about why you're here over dinner.
Uh, okay.

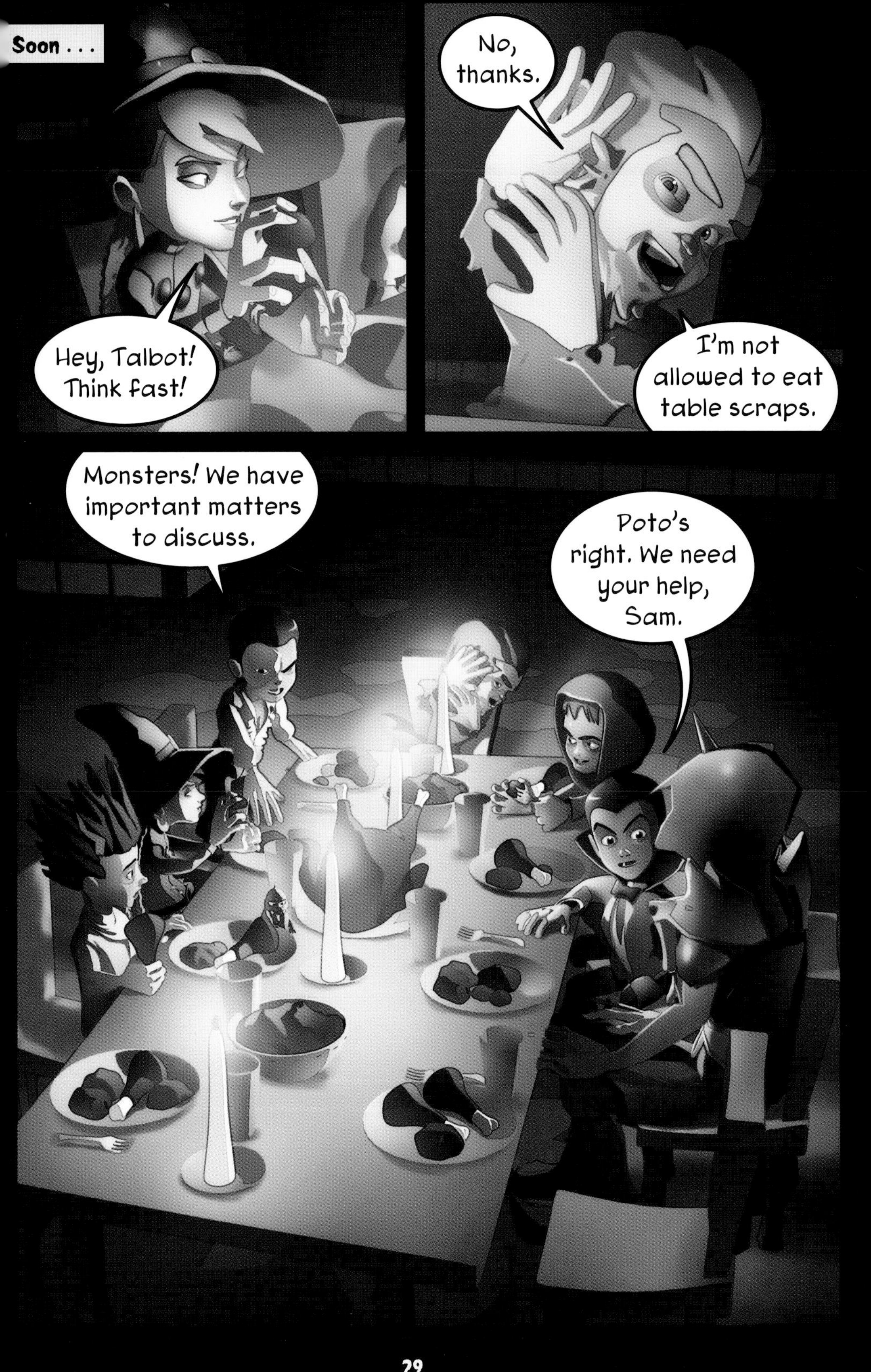
Soon . . .
Hey, Talbot! Think fast!
No, thanks.
I'm not allowed to eat table scraps.
Monsters! We have important matters to discuss.
Poto's right. We need your help, Sam.

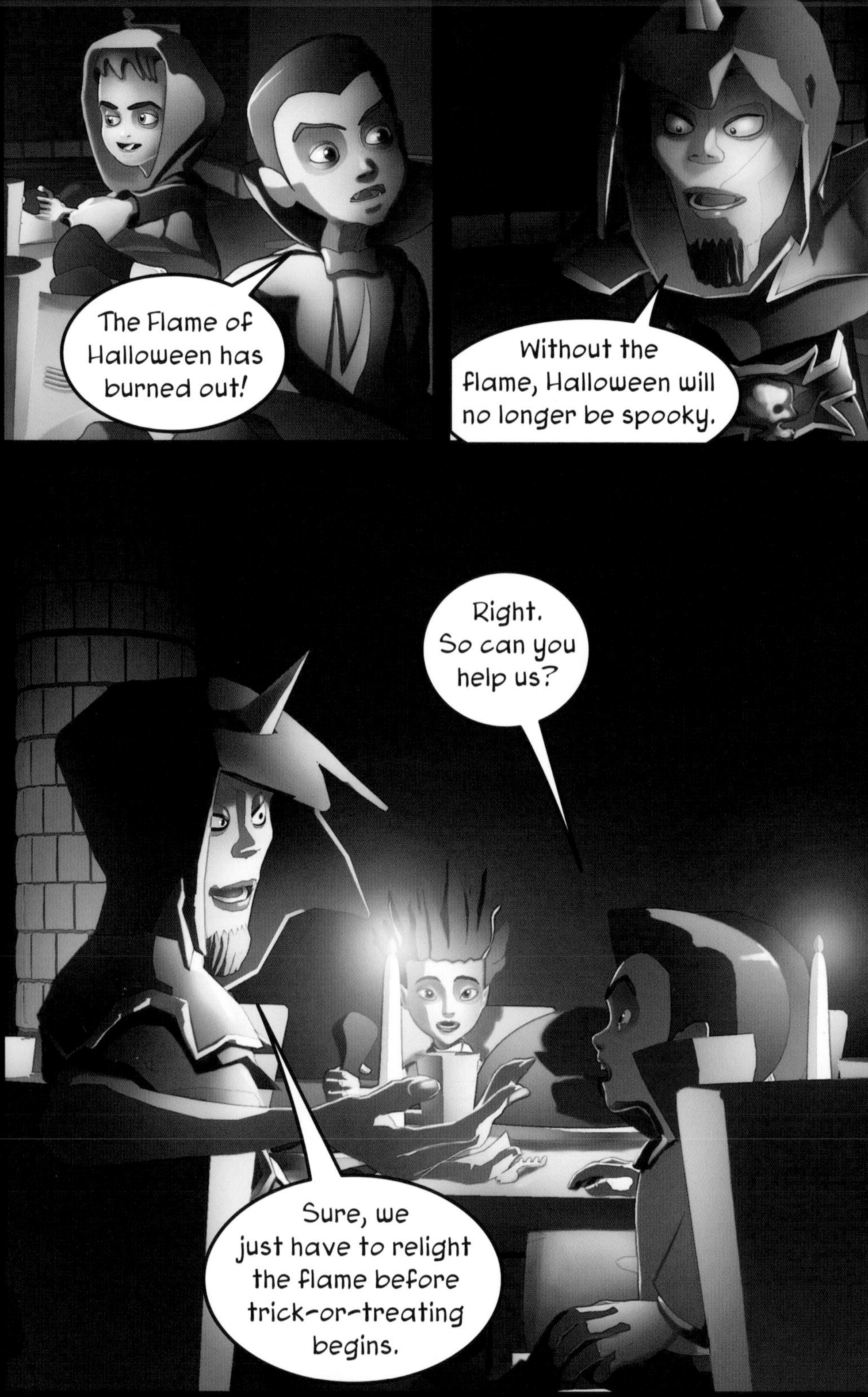
The Flame of Halloween has burned out!
Without the flame, Halloween will no longer be spooky.
Right. So can you help us?
Sure, we just have to relight the flame before trick-or-treating begins.

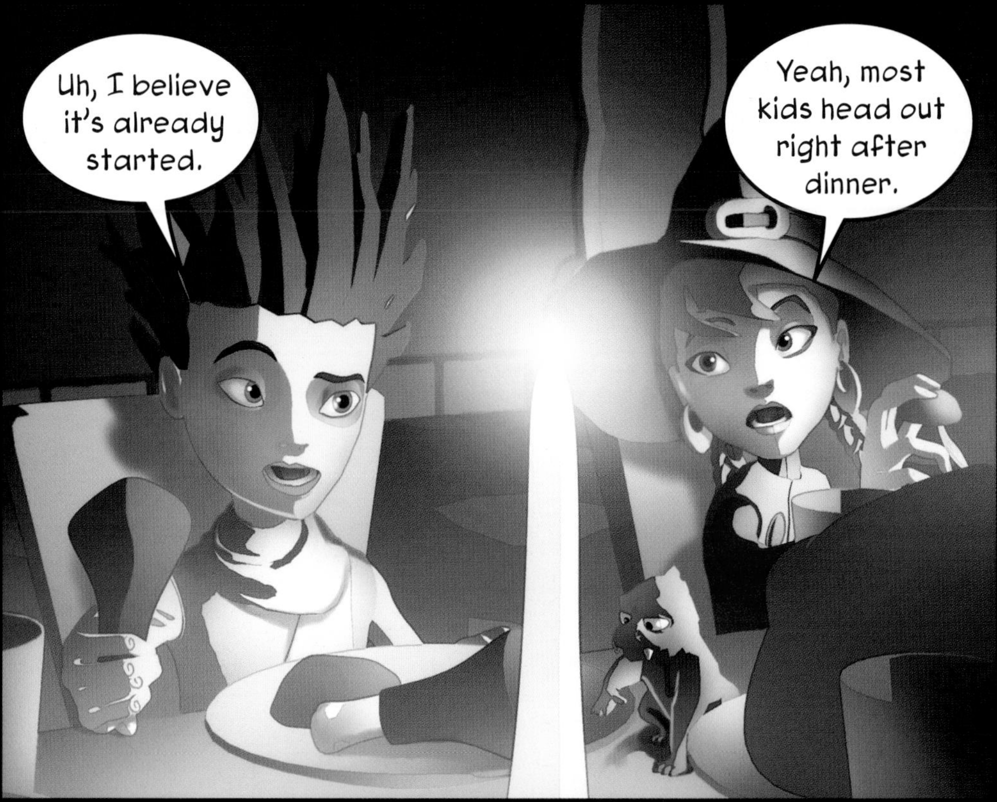
Uh, I believe it's already started.
Yeah, most kids head out right after dinner.

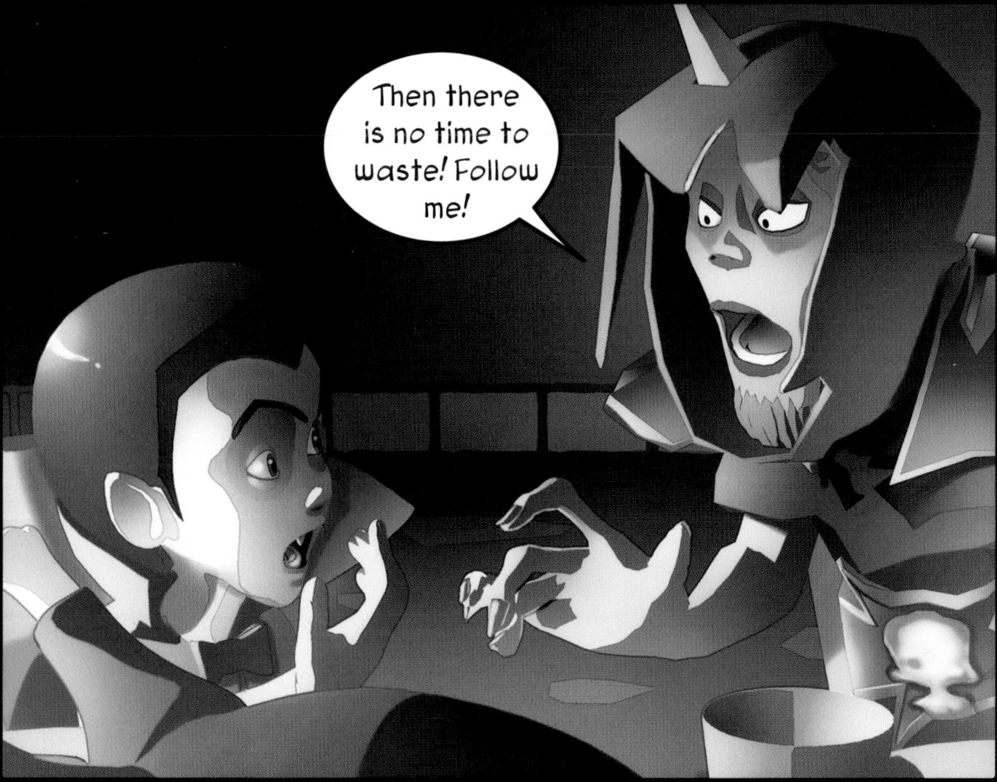
Then there is no time to waste! Follow me!

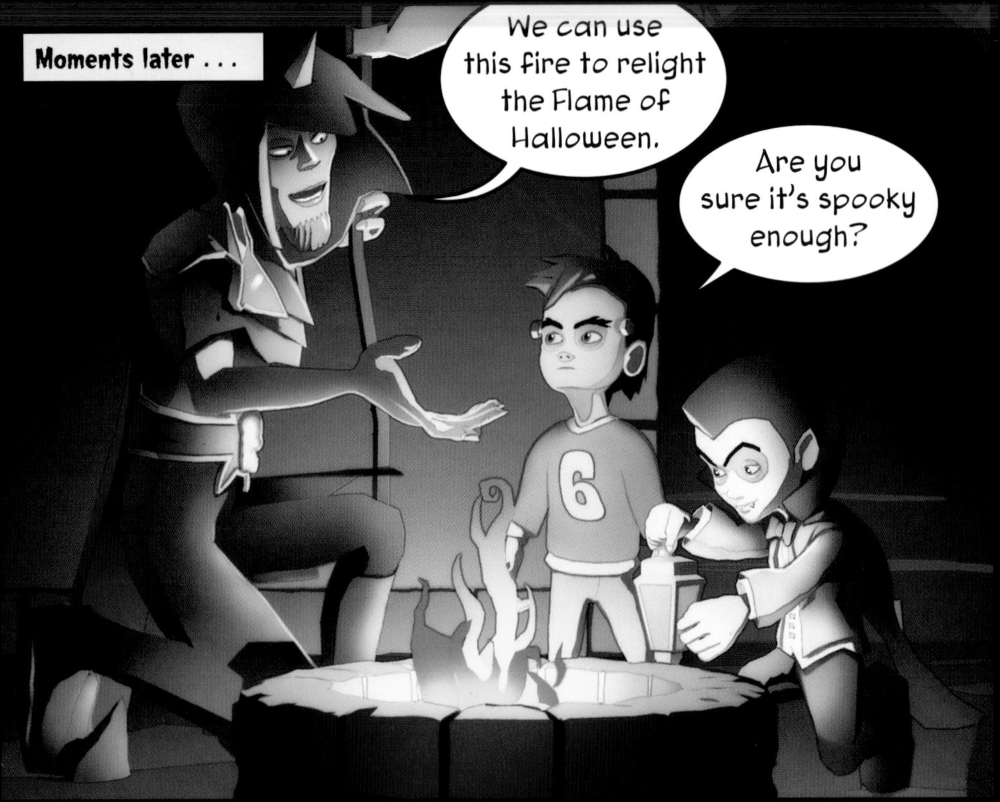
Moments later . . .
We can use this fire to relight the Flame of Halloween.
Are you sure it's spooky enough?

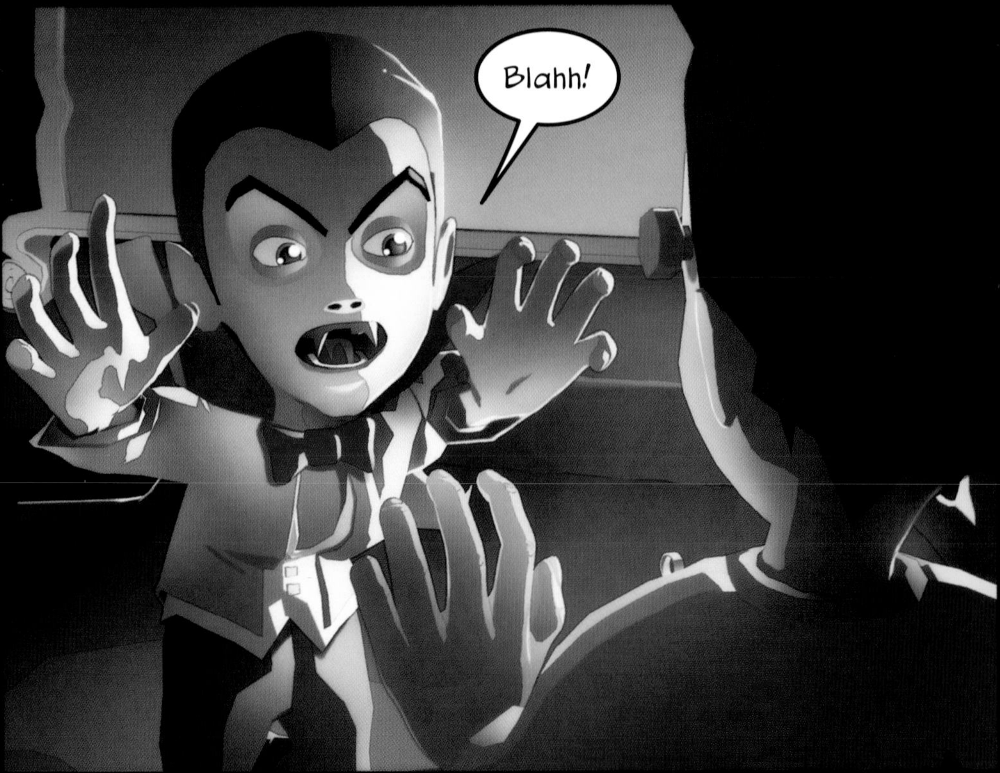
Blahh!

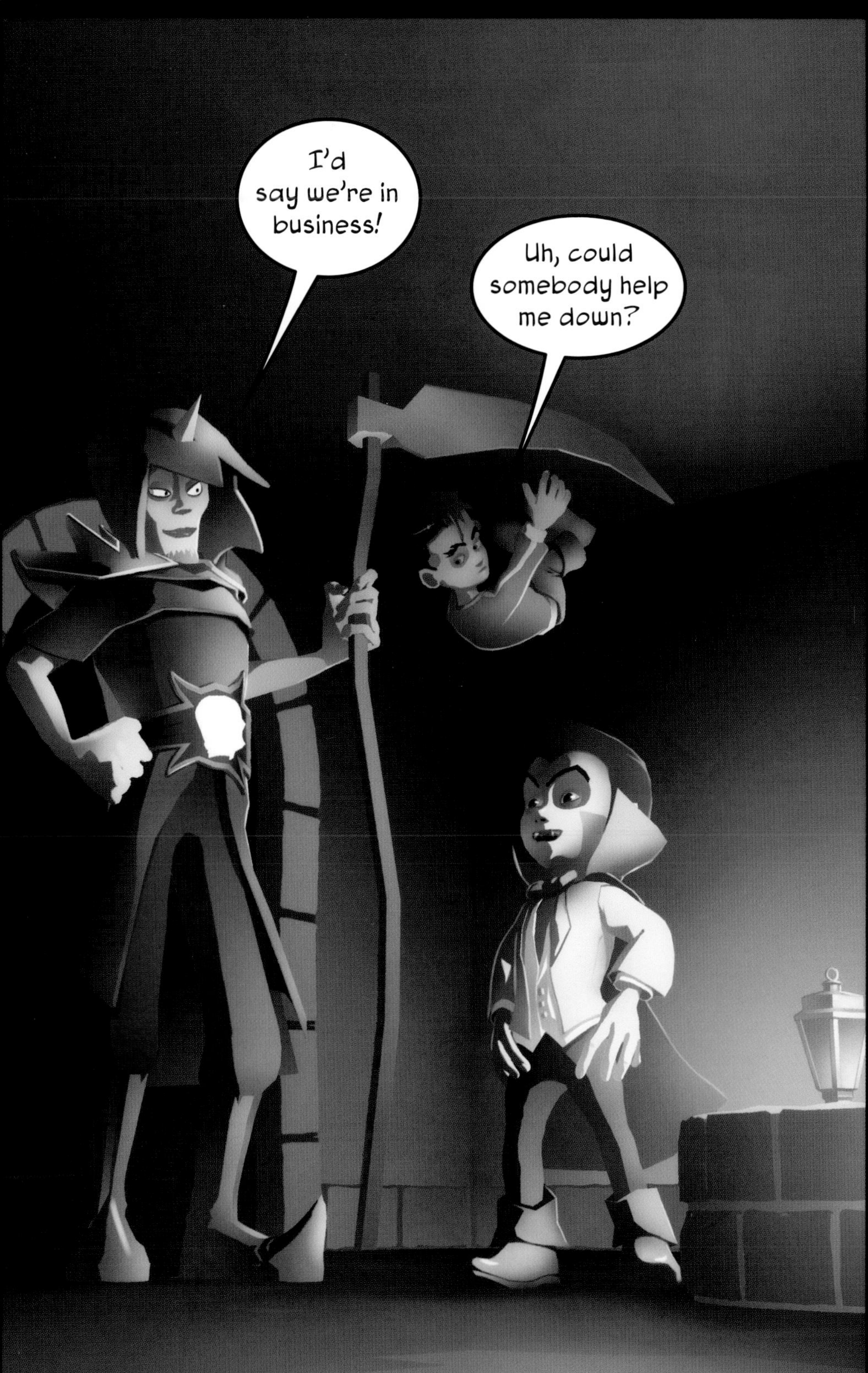
I'd say we're in business!
Uh, could somebody help me down?

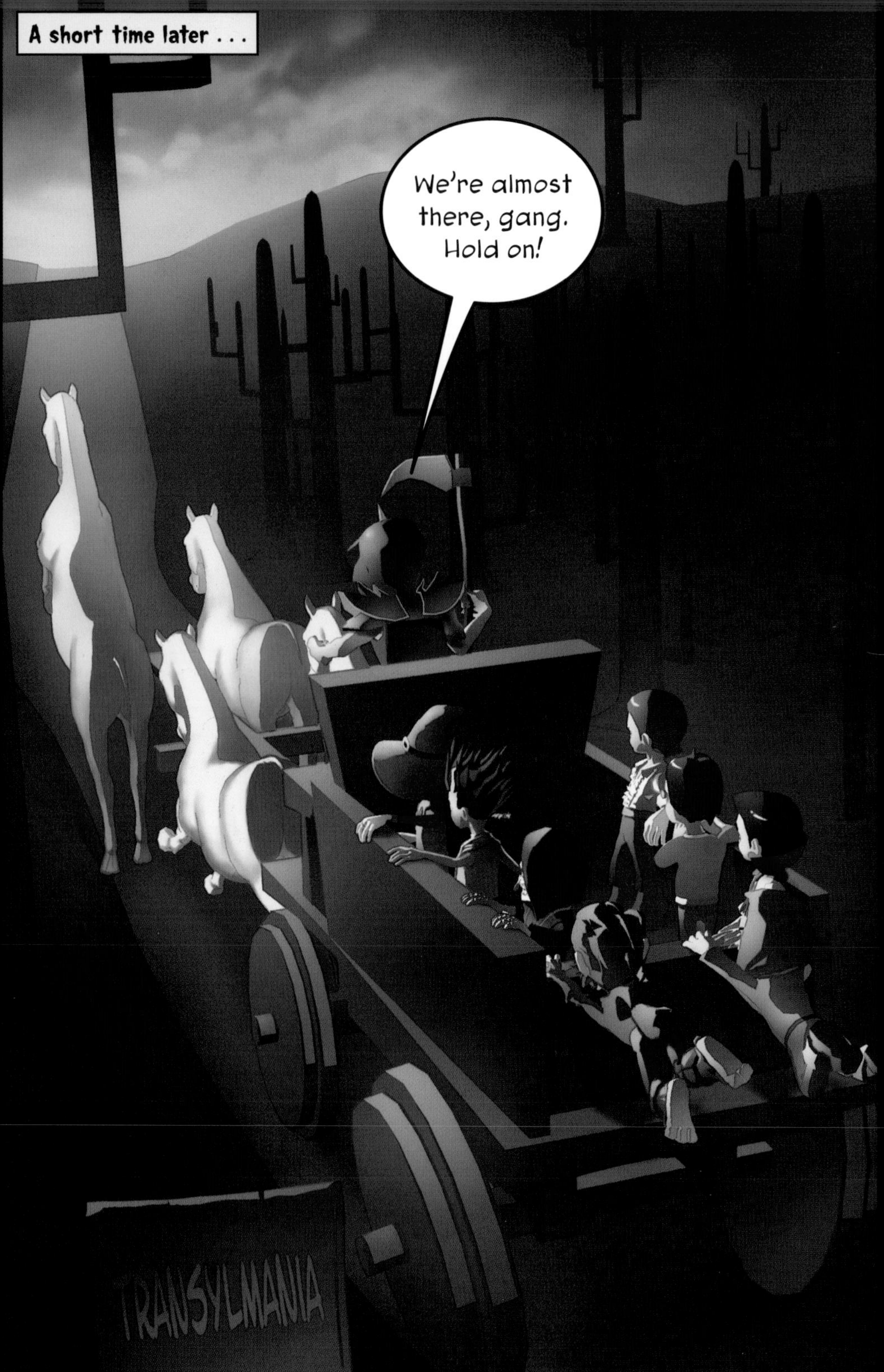
A short time later . . .
We're almost there, gang. Hold on!
TRANSYLMANIA

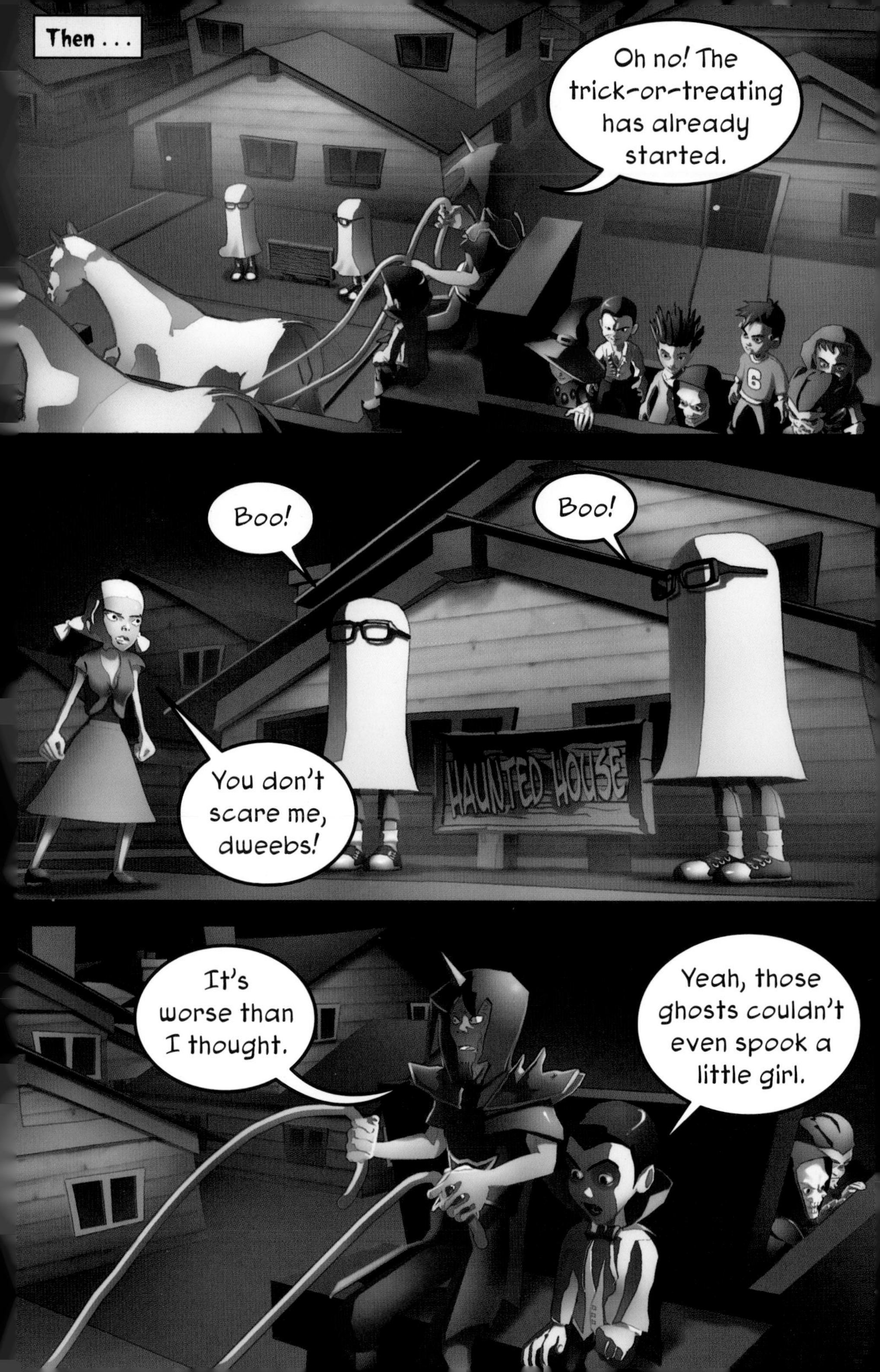
Then . . .
Oh no! The trick-or-treating has already started.
Boo!
Boo!
You don't scare me, dweebs!
HAUNTED HOUSE
It's worse than I thought.
Yeah, those ghosts couldn't even spook a little girl.

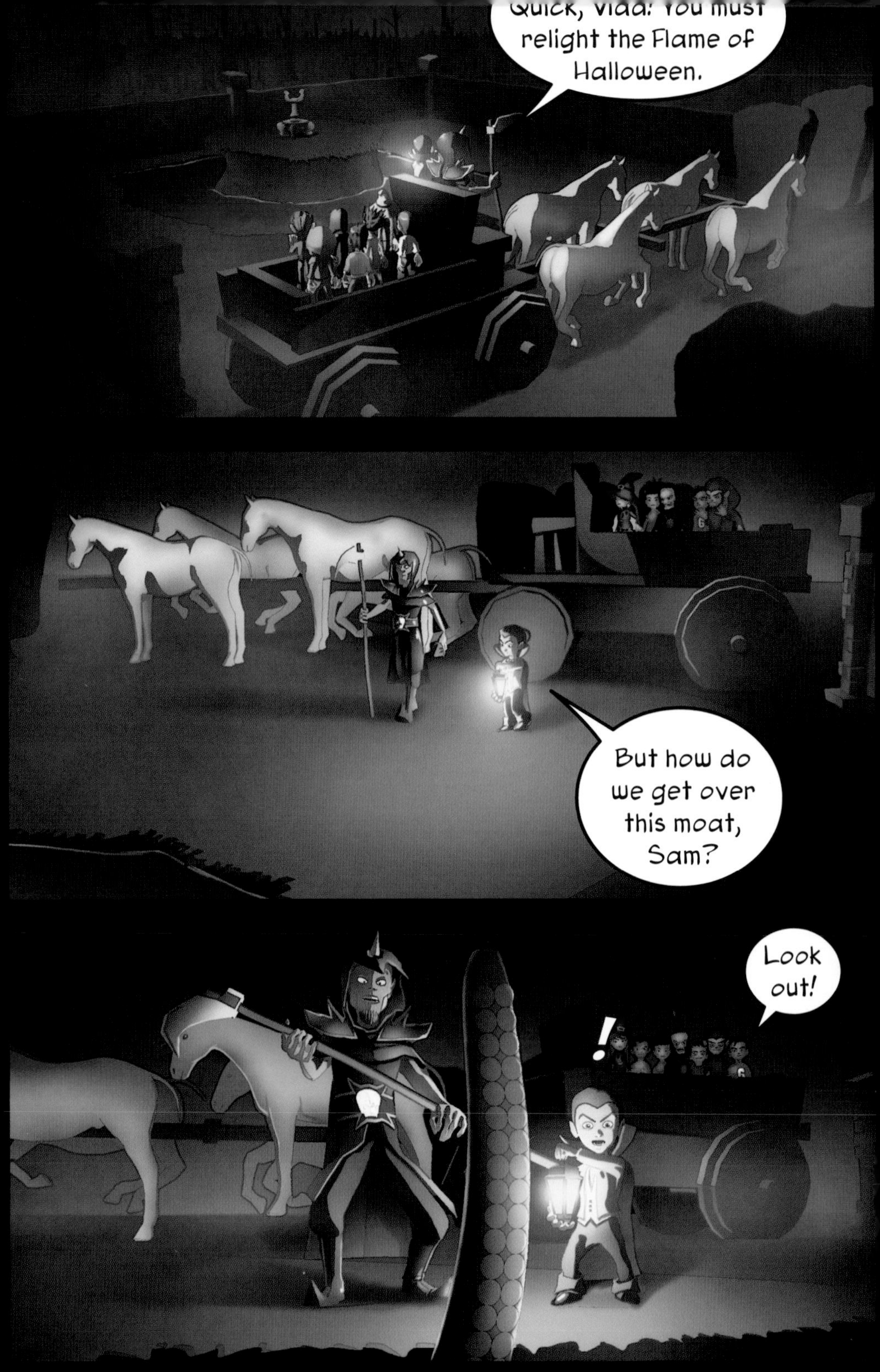
Quick, Vlad! You must
relight the Flame of
Halloween.
But how do
we get over
this moat,
Sam?
Look
out!

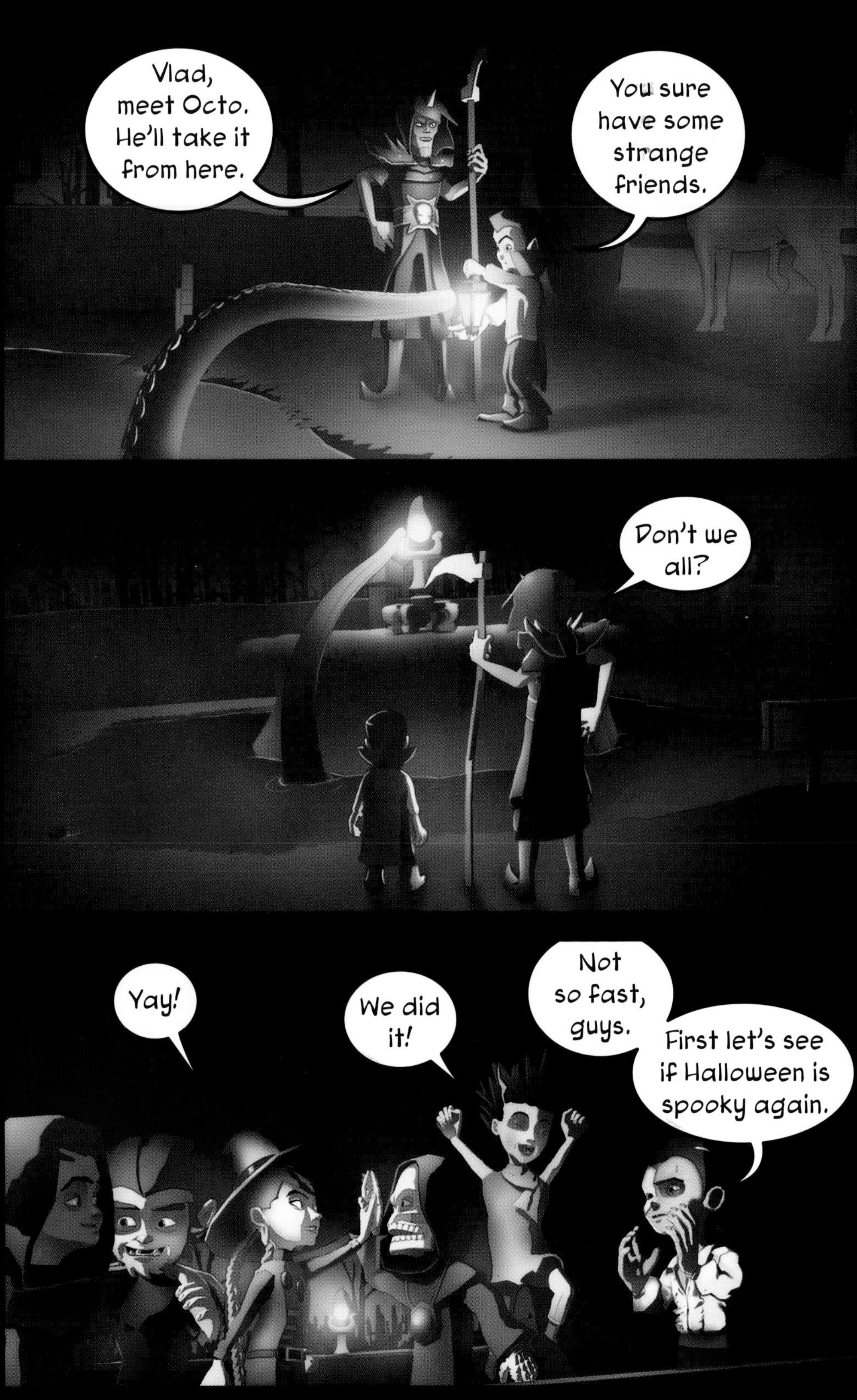
Vlad, meet Octo. He'll take it from here.
You sure have some strange friends.
Don't we all?
Yay!
We did it!
Not so fast, guys.
First let's see if Halloween is spooky again.

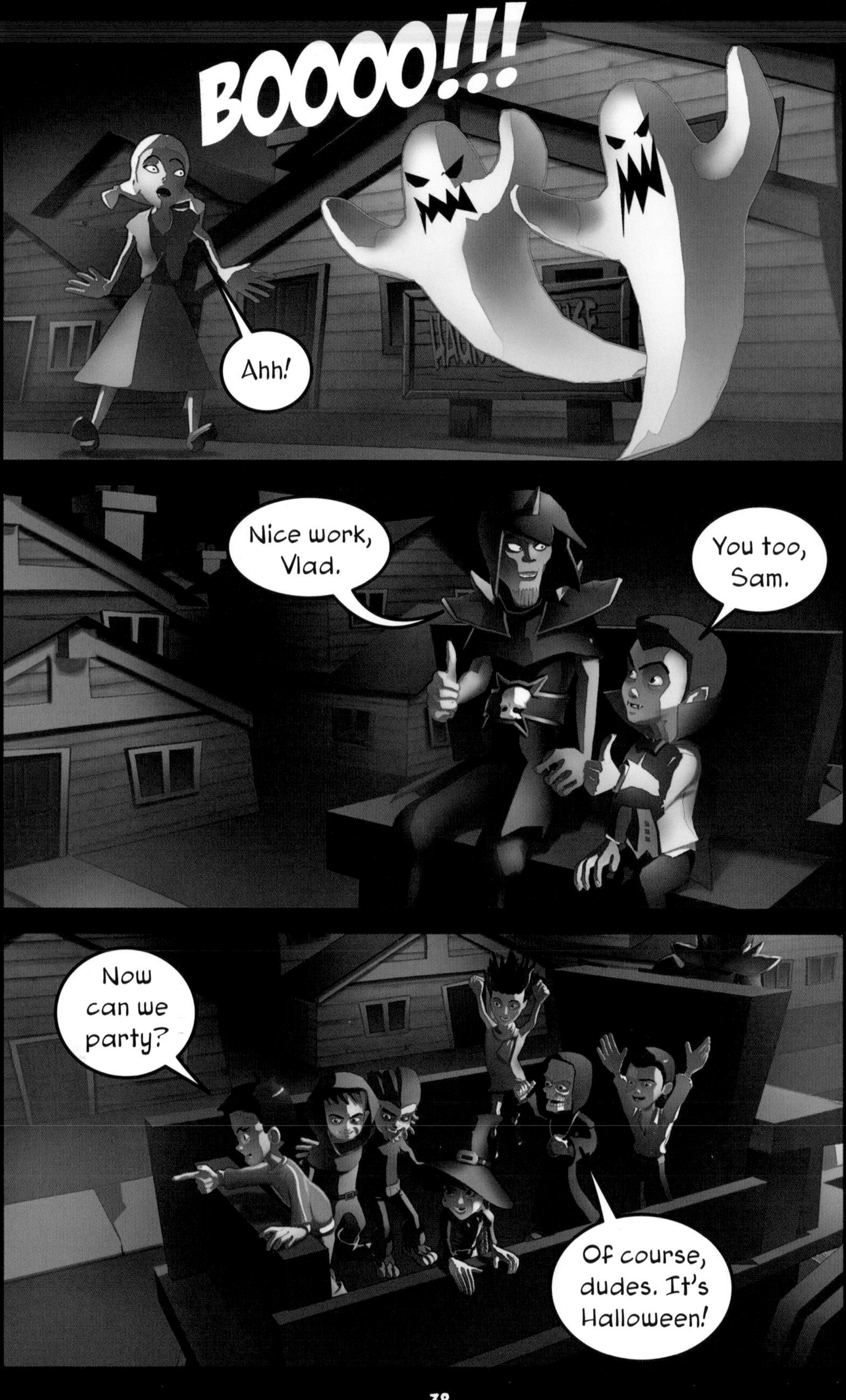
BOOOO!!!
Ahh!
Nice work, Vlad.
You too, Sam.
Now can we party?
Of course, dudes. It's Halloween!

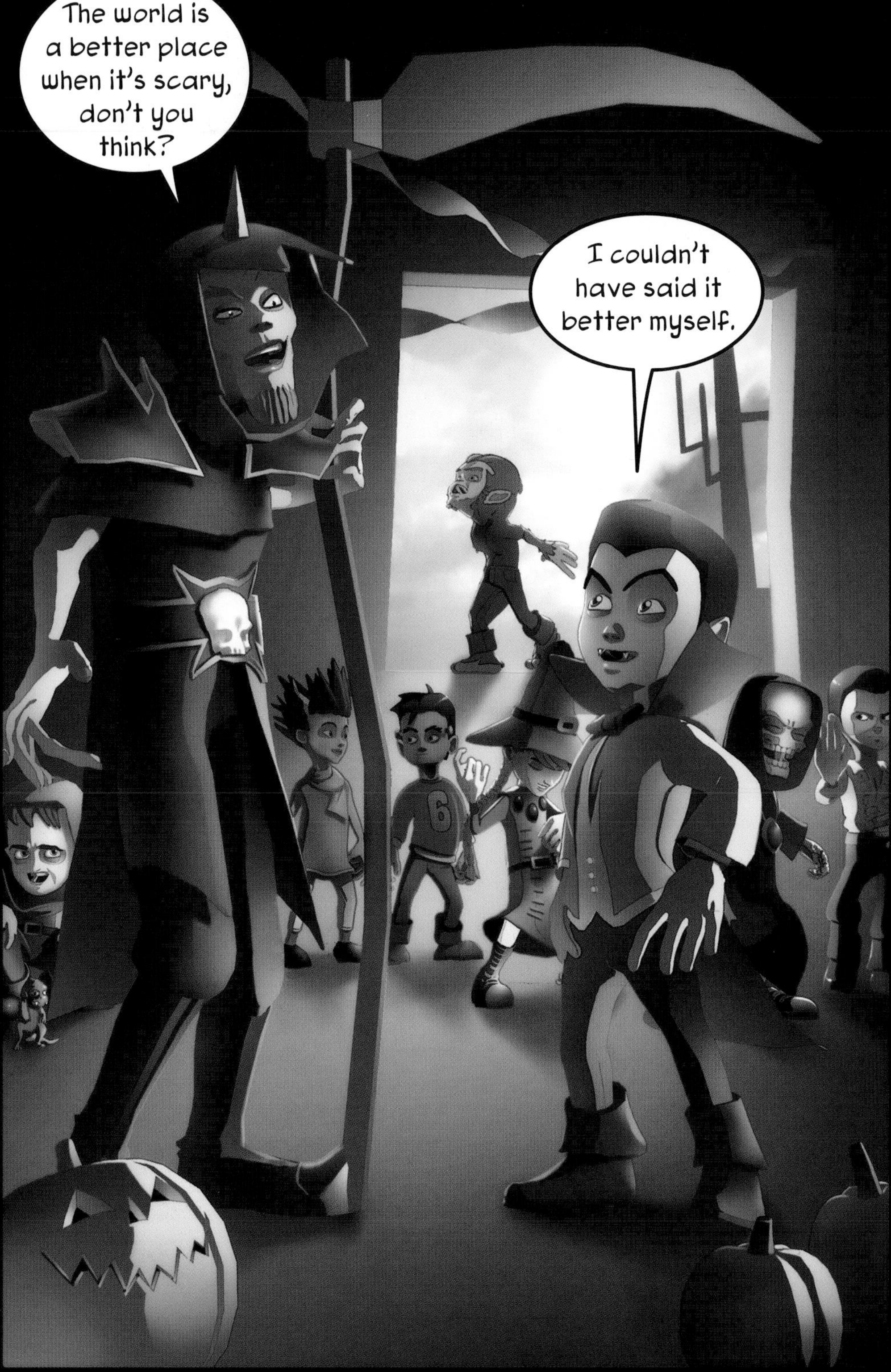
The world is a better place when it's scary, don't you think?
I couldn't have said it better myself.

Mighty Mighty Map of . . .

TRANSYLMANIA!

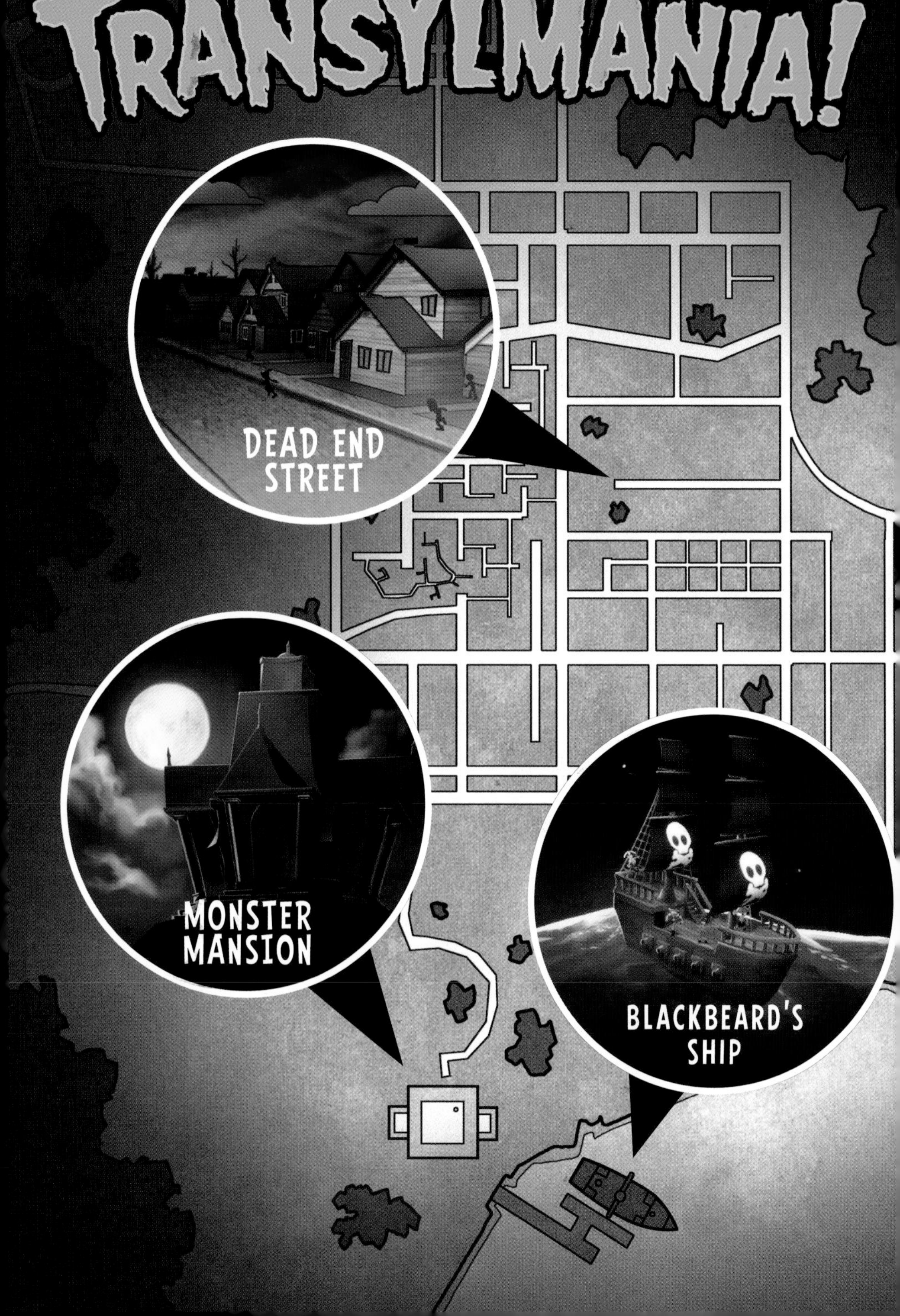
DEAD END
STREET
MONSTER
MANSION
BLACKBEARD'S
SHIP

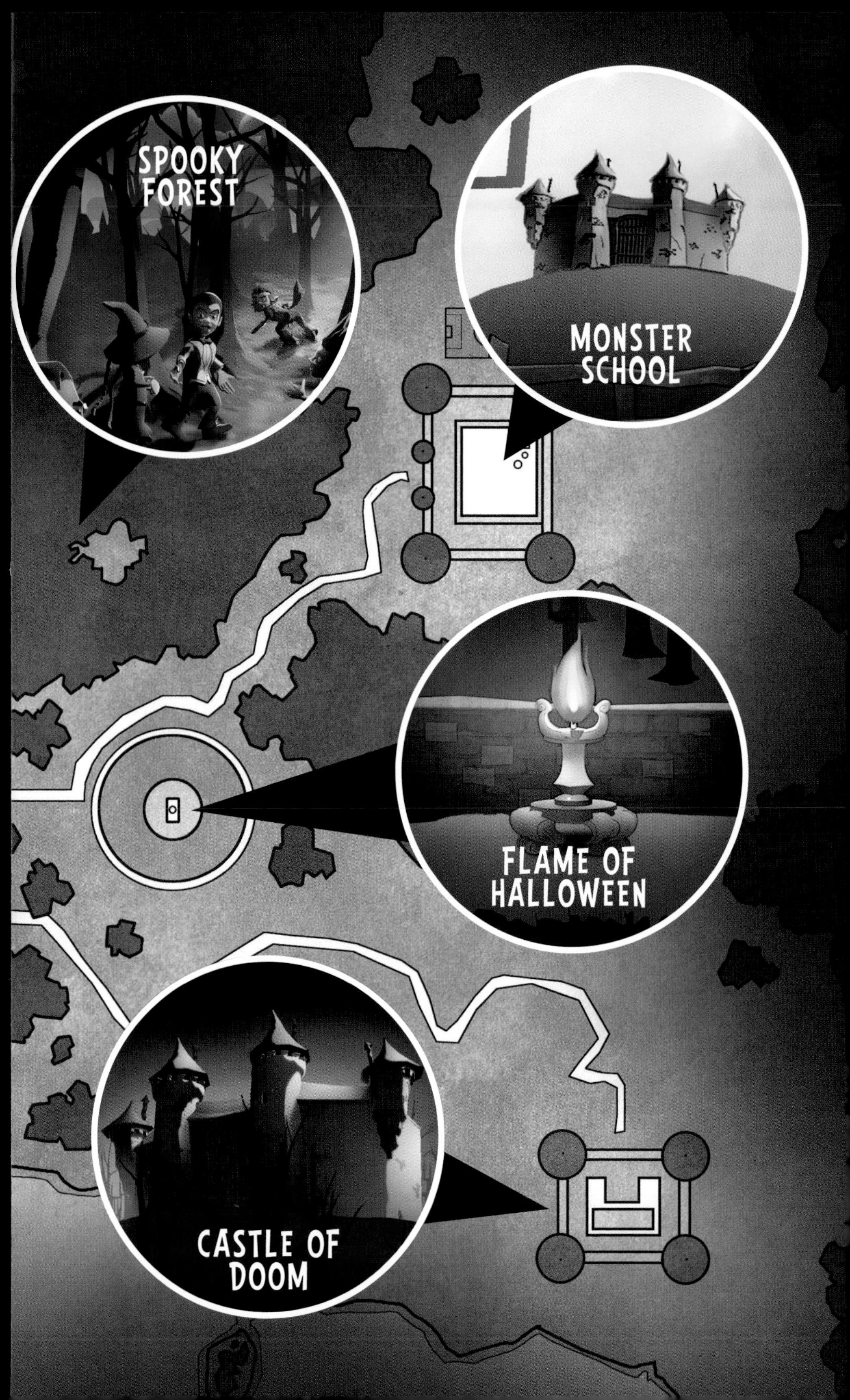
SPOOKY FOREST
MONSTER SCHOOL
FLAME OF HALLOWEEN
CASTLE OF DOOM

Mighty Mighty MONSTERS

...BEFORE THEY WERE STARS!

FRANKIE AND MARY

Nicknames: Frank and M.

Hometown: Transylmania

Favorite Colors: Red and yellow

Mighty Mighty Powers: Superhuman strength; ability to smash through concrete with a single blow; able to lift ten times their body weight; together, their powers are doubled.

BIOGRAPHIES

Growing up as neighbors in Transylmania, Frankie and Mary quickly discovered that they had more in common than green skin. Both of their parents were scientists, who "developed" their children into powerful monsters. Soon, Frank and Mary looked for a way to channel their superhuman strengths — and the Mighty Mighty Monsters were the perfect fit. Later in life, the two friends married and became Hollywood's first superpowered creature couple.

WHERE ARE THEY NOW?

In 1818, author Mary Shelley published *Frankenstein*, the first book about the famous green monster. Shelley said the idea came to her in a dream.

In 1931, actor Boris Karloff played Frankenstein in the movie of Shelley's novel. Although the monster's looks have changed many times, this became the most popular version of the creepy creature.

A few years later in 1935, studios released a sequel to the *Frankenstein* movie titled *The Bride of Frankenstein*. In this film, the green beast is finally married.

About Sean O'Reilly
and Arcana Studio

As a lifelong comics fan, Sean O'Reilly dreamed of becoming a comic book creator. In 2004, he realized that dream by creating Arcana Studio. In one short year, O'Reilly took his studio from a one-person operation in his basement to an award-winning comic book publisher with more than 150 graphic novels produced for Harper Collins, Simon & Schuster, Random House, Scholastic, and others.

Within a year, the company won many awards including the Shuster Award for Outstanding Publisher and the Moonbeam Award for top children's graphic novel. O'Reilly also won the Top 40 Under 40 award from the city of Vancouver and authored The Clockwork Girl for Top Graphic Novel at Book Expo America in 2009.

Currently, O'Reilly is one of the most prolific independent comic book writers in Canada. While showing no signs of slowing down in comics, he now writes screenplays and adapts his creations for the big screen.

GLOSSARY

amuse (uh-MYOOz)—to make someone laugh or smile

collector (kuh-LEK-tor)—one who collects something as a hobby

electrifying (ih-LEK-tri-fy-ing)—the act of shocking something with electricity or making someone excited

hobby (HOB-ee)—something that you enjoy doing in your spare time

introduce (in-truh-DOOSS)—to cause to be known by name

moat (MOHT)—a deep, wide ditch dug around a fort, castle, or town and filled with water to prevent attacks

nickname (NIK-name)—a descriptive name used with, or instead of, a person's real name

passage (PASS-ij)—a hall or corridor

solution (suh-LOO-shuhn)—the answer to a problem

terror (TER-ur)—very great fear

torture (TOR-chur)—extreme pain or mental suffering

DISCUSSION QUESTIONS

1. Before they met Samhain, the Mighty Mighty Monsters were afraid of him. Have you ever judged someone without actually meeting them? Explain.

2. The Mighty Mighty Monsters are a team. Who do you think is the leader? Do you think every team needs a leader? Explain.

3. All of the Mighty Mighty Monsters are different. Which character do you like the best? Why?

WRITING PROMPTS

1. Imagine a brand new member of the Mighty Mighty Monsters. What superpowers would your monster have? What would it look like? Write about your Mighty Mighty Monster, and then draw a picture of it.

2. Write a story about your favorite Halloween. Where did you go? What costume did you wear? What kinds of candy did you get?

3. Write your own Mighty Mighty Monsters adventure. What will the ghoulish gang do next? What villains will they face? You decide.

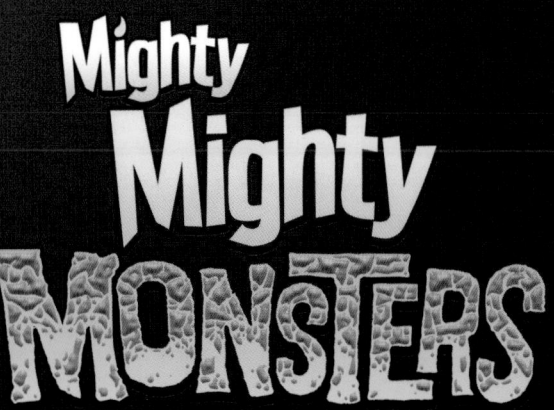

Mighty Mighty MONSTERS ADVENTURES

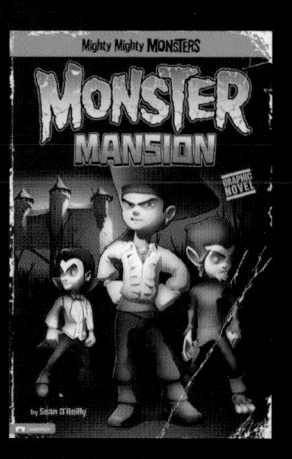

Mighty Mighty MONSTERS
MONSTER MANSION
GRAPHIC NOVEL
by Sean O'Reilly

Monster Mansion

Mighty Mighty MONSTERS
NEW MONSTER in SCHOOL
GRAPHIC NOVEL
by Sean O'Reilly

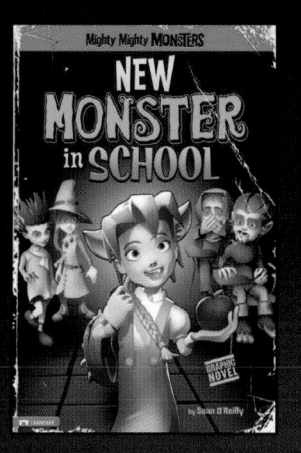

New Monster in School

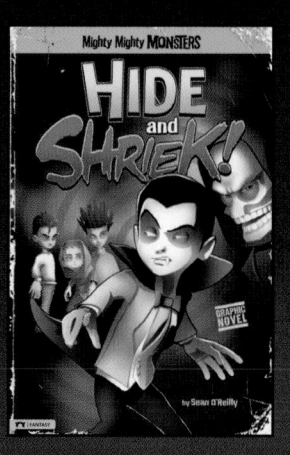

Mighty Mighty MONSTERS
HIDE and SHRIEK!
GRAPHIC NOVEL
by Sean O'Reilly

Hide and Shriek

Mighty Mighty MONSTERS
My MISSING MONSTER
by Sean O'Reilly
GRAPHIC NOVEL

My Missing Monster

Mighty Mighty MONSTERS
Lost in SPOOKY FOREST
by Sean O'Reilly
GRAPHIC NOVEL

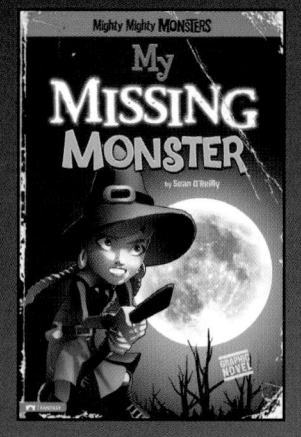

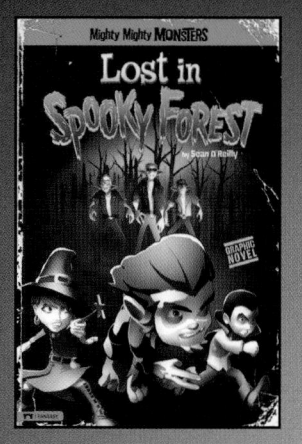

Lost in Spooky Forest

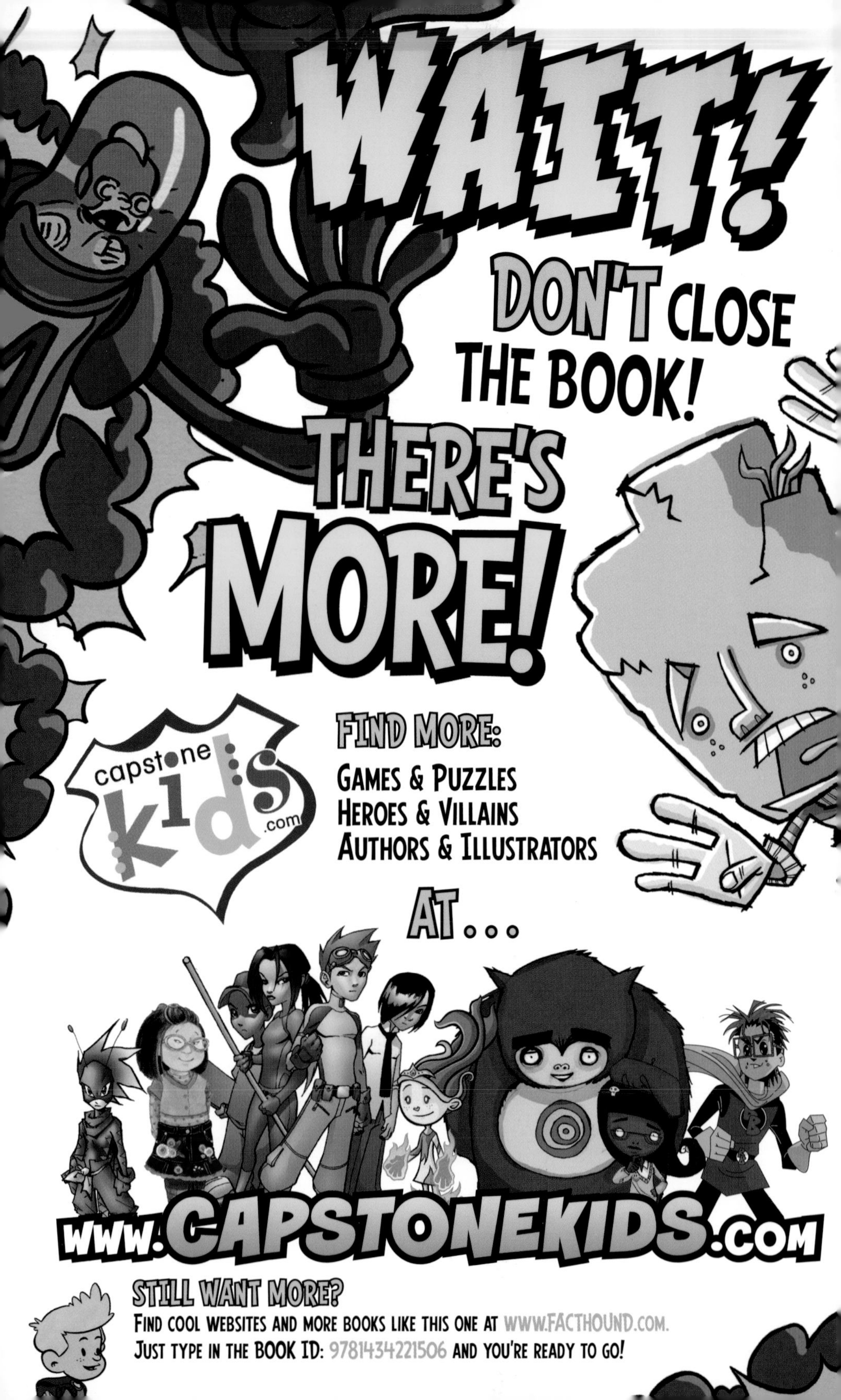
WAIT!
DON'T CLOSE THE BOOK!
THERE'S MORE!
capstone kids .com
FIND MORE:
GAMES & PUZZLES
HEROES & VILLAINS
AUTHORS & ILLUSTRATORS
AT...
WWW.CAPSTONEKIDS.COM
STILL WANT MORE?
FIND COOL WEBSITES AND MORE BOOKS LIKE THIS ONE AT WWW.FACTHOUND.COM.
JUST TYPE IN THE BOOK ID: 9781434221506 AND YOU'RE READY TO GO!